The Psychosis of

Alice Petalow

The Psychosis of

Alice Petalow

P W Stephens

Published by PWS

© Copyright P W Stephens 2020

THE PSYCHOSIS OF
ALICE PETALOW

ISBN 978–1-703-93209-6

Book formatted by www.bookformatting.co.uk.

Contents

Authors Note

I remember a time before you, before the doubt and before the pain. I remember a time when my skin wasn't laced with scars and when the creature at the bottom of my bed had no voice. It was a time when I was too young to realise why I felt so constantly numb, why I felt so alone; and then you changed that, you changed me. But I know now, I know that I had an illness. I know that it became stronger when I found something in my life that I was reluctant to lose. But I must admit it was your arrival in my world that gave the creature its voice. I had nothing before you entered my life, so it's just a shame that it followed you through the open door to my heart. I have survived Jacob Brooking, but I am no less haunted by Thomas Levit.

Acknowledgements

Thank you to my family and friends for your unwavering support.

To the whole of team Stephens…

To Kimberly and Susan for taking my book multinational.

To my mother, for never judging me on my many failures and loving me along each troubled path.

To Lucy, who bought and read my book before all others.

To Maria, who pulled me through my writer's block when all hope seemed lost.

To my Grace Natasha, who remains my guiding light. You are more than a daughter to me; you are my world.

To Jacqueline, Kay and Samara, for helping develop the plot twist that even I couldn't see coming.

And to Edgar Allan Poe, for inspiring me to write in such a manner that my audience is captivated (hopefully) by not knowing all the facts until the very end of the book, and sometimes beyond.

.

To the men that I love – Jamie, David, Jack and Max.

Thank you for your endless support.

And then, Alice awoke… Alice who had been lying deadly still on the hospital bed for what had seemed like years. The room was clinical and open, with nothing inside it that didn't have a purpose. She lay on her side, crunched into a foetal position, with just one white pillow folded beneath her plaited auburn hair.

The end of *The Rise and Fall of Jacob Brooking*

Prologue: The Lighthouse

Song of the day: 'Let's Dance'
by David Bowie

Jacob couldn't decide on a way forward. This was a pivotal decision, one that had to be made with a clear mind and a calm heart. If he hung out the washing on the east-wing line, it would surely dry better away from the sea mist; but those bloody crows – damn those bloody crows – they always left mess all over that side of the grounds, and they cared little for the brilliant white of his T-shirts. The west wing was getting increasingly hit by ever-more-aggressive waves smashing against the coast. The ocean spray lashed hard against the white stone walls of the lighthouse, like a giant primordial lash, bringing a thunderous clap like shingle thrown onto a tin roof with each giant splash. Jacob was unsure how long he had been living on this gargantuan rock surrounded by a violent sea and a murder of monstrous crows, but he knew he was happy and that this place almost defined him, with its melting pot of beauty and uncontrolled environmental destruction. It was as if someone who knew Jacob intimately had created this place for him. 'The east wing,' he murmured to himself, knowing he was taking a chance. He carried the wicker laundry basket across the lush green of the lighthouse's back yard and over to the wood house, where the washing line sat loosely on the ground.

'KRAAAAAA,' the closest crow called from the large birch tree that the other end of the line would attach to.

'Kraa yourself, you big bag of feathers!' Jacob responded.

As Jacob pegged his clothes on the line, his attention was pulled back to the lighthouse. He swore he could hear his father calling from the kitchen. *Maybe lunch is ready*, he mused while he hurried his pace, eager to see what his dad had created for a well-earned break in play. They had a good system here. Paul Brooking would wash the clothes, while Jacob hung them out; his dad would cook lunch, while Jacob always made dinner; and Paul loved to tend the garden, while his son looked after the welfare of the lighthouse itself – not that they had ever seen a ship to warn. Jacob hadn't yet figured out how this place worked or even if it had a name. But they had made it a home, and they were happy. The larder was somehow always full, and although the weather threatened, it had always been kind.

'I'm coming, Pops,' called Jacob as he pegged up the last shirt. He looked up briefly to warn the crows that any attempt to ruin his work would involve grave consequences, but to his amazement, not a feather could be seen. In fact, he couldn't see a bird in the sky. 'Not even a gull to ruin my washing. Maybe my luck's in.' Jacob smiled, picked up the empty wicker basket and began his stroll back to the lighthouse so as to enjoy another five-star lunch with his best friend.

'Son, I've been calling you,' said Jacob's dad as he put a platter of cured meats and smoked cheeses down on a giant oak chopping board at the centre of a circular table.

'Dad, this looks beautiful,' said Jacob, taking his place in a chair next to a sleeping Peepo. The black Lab had been waiting for them at the window the day they'd arrived, and Jacob had to admit that his heart had lifted immeasurably to see her beautiful shiny wet nose at the window as his father had led them along the beach to what would become their new home.

'Hold on, son, the best is yet to come.' Paul Brooking pulled a loaf of rosemary bread from the Aga. Steam and herb-filled aromas filled the kitchen, and an almost incandescent glow radiated off the bread. Paul laid it down next to a dish of sea-salted butter and smiled.

'Dad, you never cease to amaze me. This all looks bloody lovely, and Mum would be proud if she were here.'

Jacob pulled a slice of ham from the table and slipped it to Peepo, who instantly pricked up her ears as Jacob whispered encouragement to the forever-starving beast.

'You can wash your hands again if you insist on feeding that bloody dog,' said Paul without even turning around.

Jacob laughed. 'What exactly am I going to catch from not washing my hands in this place?'

'What exactly do you think this place is, my boy?'

'Oh, sweet Jesus, Dad, you know I can't answer that. The words always seem to escape me even as I try to speak them, and honestly, Pop, haven't we been through this little dance enough times?' Jacob, although defiant in his reasons, was still a son who did as his father asked, and so he jumped to his feet, sinking his hands into the soapy water Paul had got ready for the plates in advance. 'You know, Dad, I've never cared where this place is, or even what our purpose here may be, but I'm truly glad I'm here with you and Peepo.'

As he went to sit back down, he noticed that Peepo had vanished. Where she had gone in a closed room of this size was a mystery, but Jacob gave it little thought, as, honestly, where could she go?

Jacob and his father ate everything at the table except for a few crusts, which were for the nest of swallows above the barn gate, and a few scraps of meat for Peepo, if and when she ever returned from her mysterious hiding place.

'Let me help you with that,' said Jacob as his dad tirelessly cleared all the plates. He reached across the table to grab the empty glasses, when something happened that shocked him frozen. 'Dad! What's happening?'

Paul looked around to see his son's left hand slowly disintegrate into an ashen vapour trail that left a mist of fireflies dancing out of existence.

The glass remained unmoved by Jacob's efforts to take it, and the fear was spreading through him like the flame that tore away at his arm.

'DAD, I'M SCARED! WHAT IS HAPPENING?'

Jacob was in full panic mode as the fire spread up his arm and into his shoulder. Each limb disappeared as the flames consumed him, as though he were a sheet of paper. Jacob looked up at his father to see him all but disappear himself.

'Don't be scared, son, you must have known this was coming.'

'What was coming? Dad, what was coming?'

Paul Brooking smiled at his son as he finally vanished. 'I love you, son, but you didn't really think this was real, did you?'

Jacob looked down as the last of his visual self finally vanished into nothing, and a veil of darkness washed over him.

He felt no pain. And he felt no peace. Jacob Brooking, by all accounts, felt nothing.

Part Three
The Dot and the Mirror

Chapter 1: Wide Eyes and William

**Song of the day: 'A Whiter Shade of Pale'
by Annie Lennox**

Summer 2009

St Martin's Hospital, Canterbury, Kent, UK

'William,' Alice croaked as she woke with the throat of a woman who hadn't uttered a word in two years.

The man in question stood with his back to Alice on the far side of the room, mid-conversation with one of the nurses, and he didn't even flinch at the frail voice that had escaped her. Alice pulled herself up with great unease, and the nurse drew William's attention to the patient.

'Alice, you're awake,' the doctor said as he hurried eagerly to her bedside.

'William, what's going on? Where am I, and what on earth are you wearing?' asked Alice, gently pulling his stethoscope.

The doctor smiled a toothy grin through his grey beard and shone a pen light into Alice's deep blue eyes. 'So many questions, Miss Petalow, and we can answer them all, but for now please just breathe and let me take a look at you. Two years is a very long time to be in and out of a catatonic state.'

Alice's heart rate increased and her breathing followed suit as the confusion started to overwhelm her. 'WILLIAM, WHAT'S GOING ON?'

The doctor leaned in once more. 'Alice, who exactly do you

think I am? You keep calling me William. Is that someone you want me to contact?'

The nurse came to take Alice's pulse. Alice sat shaking as she tried to piece her world back together.

'You're William, my boyfriend,' she said. 'You just told me you loved me whilst on our first weekend away.'

The doctor raised his hand. 'Alice, I'm not William, I'm Dr Williams, and I've been overseeing your stay here at the hospital for the past 23 months.' The doctor pulled up his security pass from the lanyard round his neck and presented it to Alice.

'Consultant J. Williams… No, NO, I don't understand.' Alice's voice started to fail as her throat fell into an uncontrollable tremble. 'WILLIAM. WHAT IS HAPPENING TO ME?'

He's not listening to you

The voice came from nowhere, and Alice barely registered it anyway.

'Alice, we need you to breathe,' said the doctor, while the nurse called for support.

He's forgotten you

He's going to leave you, just like Jacob did

'Jacob,' Alice murmured on hearing the name voiced in her head. She rocked back and forth, struggling to control her breathing like the doctor had asked.

'Do you need Jacob?' the doctor answered. 'We will call him as soon as you settle, he was just here yesterday.'

'WHAT?' Alice stopped hyperventilating. 'But Jacob's dead.'

She hadn't used her legs in two years, and her attempt at making it to the toilet was futile to say the least. Dr Williams tried to catch her, but Alice still took a rather nasty hit to her knee as her legs immediately buckled, like those of a newborn giraffe trying to find its footing, and she hit the ground.

Alice opened her mouth to breathe for what felt like the first time since the doctor had told her the news. But she struggled to draw in anything of sustenance and started to suffocate, despite there being no restriction on her airway.

'Breathe, Alice, you need to calm down.'

'MY DEAD HUSBAND IS APPARENTLY NOW ALIVE AND MY NEW BOYFRIEND, WHO APPARENTLY IS NOT MY BOYFRIEND AT ALL, IS THE DOCTOR TELLING ME ALL THIS,' Alice screeched while gulping huge breaths in between each and every word. She bellowed once more, 'And YOU – YOU, who looks identical to the man who just today, as sunrise touched my eyes and awoke me from dreams, told me he loved me, as he kissed me gently good morning – YOU, of all people, want me, ME, to calm down?'

Alice was overwhelmed and emptied her stomach of whatever protein-rich fluid had been pumped into her these past two years with the sole purpose of keeping her alive. Her world went to darkness once again, and the last of her strength slipped away into nothing. The only remnants of consciousness in her weary and broken form came from a tiny twitch she made every time she heard the voice in her head call out to her.

Alice, come back to us!

Chapter 2: Scar Tissue

Song of the day: 'No Surprises' by Radiohead

Summer 2009

St Martin's Hospital, Canterbury, Kent, UK

Alice hadn't spoken in minutes, but Dr Vivian Phillips didn't have any desire to rush her through this; after all, she wasn't on the clock today. She had been brought in especially. Alice's parents had paid a handsome sum to make sure Alice got all the help she needed from a doctor who knew her personally and had experience with her broken past.

'So, I've been in an induced coma since I cut my throat?' Alice asked.

'Not quite. We pulled you out of it as soon as your stitches healed fully. You were induced because you wouldn't stop trying to tear them out. You nearly bled out on us twice, Alice.' The doctor held back a genuine sadness at the fall of her favourite client and pushed some photos across the desk.

The images showed Alice on the same hospital bed she had woken up on not a day before.

'But these photos show I'm wide awake,' said Alice as she flipped through the pictures, which were dated by month starting a year earlier.

'When you were taken out of the coma, you remained in an unresponsive catatonic state for a further 12 months. We could get nothing from you other than one thing.'

The doctor slid one last photograph across the table and placed a painted and finely manicured nail on the image. 'He came to see you every day for the first four months, and then every few weeks after that. He even brought you flowers on your birthday just the other day.'

'Jacob's alive,' Alice whispered.

'Yes, quite alive, although at times over these past few years, I believe he's struggled to believe that's a good thing.'

'Have you kept seeing him – you know, in a professional sense? Is he OK?'

'I believe he's on his way here now. But, Alice, it's been two years. You have to be prepared for a different Jacob to walk through that door. His therapy has been intense, but you would be so very proud of him.'

Alice found a smile for the first time since she had woken. 'But I saw him die – I held him in my arms as he bled out. What do you think that could have meant?'

The doctor smiled. 'Do you think maybe that was your way of forgiving him and letting him go?'

They sat in silence for a moment while Alice soaked in what she was hearing.

'Alice, there is one more thing we need to discuss, if you are up for it? Before we induced you, before the doctors could stop you tearing your stitches out, well, you kept screaming out a name.'

'Thomas,' Alice interrupted, with fear edging into her voice.

'Let's talk about Thomas for a little bit – that's if you're strong enough?'

'Yeah, erm... I mean, of course.' Alice sighed and looked at the floor. 'To be honest, I'm so very tired of keeping secrets designed to protect other people.' She reached up and scratched at the long-since-healed scar on her neck. Then she raised herself up and gingerly moved over to the en suite, stopping at the mirror to take a look at the horror looking back from beyond the reflection. 'But before we start, can we find a way to shut this bitch up who won't stop screaming in my head?'

Alice's reflection laughed at the audacity of such a pathetic specimen calling her a bitch and smiled a fang-toothed grin as a way of acknowledgement to Alice's true self.

Chapter 3: Ahab

Song of the day: 'Roads'
by Portishead

Summer 2009

St Martin's Hospital, Canterbury, Kent, UK

You fucking piece of shit

Jacob stood tall as his reflection voiced its unwanted opinion from the protection of a broken old mirror crudely stuck onto the men's-room door. A bigger and better mirror surely wouldn't have stretched the budget of the best private hospital in Kent.

Don't ignore me

'I'm not ignoring you, Ahab,' Jacob replied. 'I thought we were going to try getting along. Remember what Dr Phillips told us to do.'

You cannot reason with me

'Well, clearly not today, as you are being an intolerable fool, so, yes, maybe I will ignore you.'

She's better off without you

Jacob straightened his collar. 'Well, on that, old friend, we can at least agree.'

7 April, one year before

'Let me get this straight – you want me to give that bastard a name?' Jacob seemed more interested than normal, and the light in

9

his eyes shone for the first time in months. 'What, pray tell, would giving the bloody thing a name do to help me?'

'Giving it a name, Mr Brooking, will grant you two things – firstly, the ability to differentiate its voice from your own internal thoughts, and, secondly, a better degree of power, if and when you fight back.'

Jacob laughed. 'Fight back? I'm not sure I've ever won a fight against that thing, certainly not one of any consequence.'

Dr Phillips raised a perfectly kept eyebrow at Jacob and peered over her black-rimmed glasses. 'If you have never won a fight with the voice inside your head, then surely you will need all the help you can get.'

She was right, he needed help, as he had hit a bit of a rut of late. The kraken within his mind was nowhere near the threat that it had been in the years before, but it was still there each and every day. He had learned to ignore all but its most abusive barbs, yet at least once a day it would find its mark. That was fine when it was just him he had to worry about, but now there was someone else to consider.

The present

Jacob took a deep breath and placed a firm hand on the bathroom door, both fear and excitement causing his heart rate to dance like the jungle drums in a 1940s King Kong film. Jacob feared he was not the titular ape in this analogy, but rather the petrified young British explorer, out for glory but with no idea what peril lay ahead. 'You've got this, Jay.' Jacob pushed through the door and fell straight into a confident stride as he took the corridor that led to Alice's ward. He had tried to make an effort, with a crisp white shirt paired with a navy tie and matching trousers. He had brought it down a notch, into a more casual look, with an informal sleeve roll that exposed the shipwreck tattoo on the underside of his forearm, a reminder of his time lost at sea aboard the *Summer Breeze* – a reminder of a time lost to himself. He rattled as he walked the halls, with more bangles and beads than a Thai monk. He wanted to impress her, needed to impress her, not because he wanted to win her back, but because deep down he knew that this was all his fault.

'You look like the woman you should be, Miss Alice,' said the ward sister, who had been kind enough to help Alice put some make-up on.

'I look rough and you very well know it, Miss Bonnie, but thank you for trying.'

Alice walked gingerly back to her bed and, with a little help from the ward sister, managed to get herself upright against a couple of large pillows that had lost their volume after one too many Sister Bonnie pat-downs. Bonnie Belmonte was a strong woman of Antiguan descent, and her thick Caribbean accent hadn't left her over a 30-year tenure in the UK.

'You are,' she said, 'what my grandma used to say, a duppy conqueror.'

Alice giggled at the strange phrase. 'And what exactly is a duppy?'

'A duppy, my sweet girl, is a ghost, and you are a ghost conqueror.' Sister Bonnie smiled as she took Alice's hand, her beautiful white teeth separated by a gap in the centre of the top row. 'You have got this, child – on that I promise.'

Alice gave her hand a delicate squeeze. 'Can you tell me about these scars?' She pointed at the tiny marks that ran over her arms and legs.

'Those are from you rolling about the floor like a loon, in a thousand shards of broken mirror. Apparently, when Jacob carried you screaming into the San Diego ER, you were bleeding from so many small cuts that they were lost as to where the actual injury was at first.'

'And what of this big one on my belly? How did that get there? I noticed it when you helped me bathe earlier, but I was unsure if it was just my mind playing tricks on me.'

The sister took a hold of Alice's hand once more and leaned in close. 'My dear child, you really don't remember a thing, do you?'

Alice shook her head as the sister pondered how to answer.

'I think the story of that particular scar is one best told by Mr Brooking,' said Bonnie, 'for I feel I won't do the story any real justice.'

Alice let the sister's hand go and smiled softly. 'I'm sure it can't be any worse than the story that brought me here.' She ran her fingers over the hairline scar on her neck. 'Thank you, Sister.'

'You're very welcome, Miss Alice. Now be strong, for I hear footsteps on my ward floor.'

As Sister Bonnie left Alice to finish the last part of her journey alone, she passed a very nervous-looking Jacob in the doorway and took a moment to place a hand on his forearm, her midnight ebony skin contrasting with his pale colour; he clearly hadn't seen too much sun in the last two years. 'You be kind to her, child. You may have been coming in for one-way conversation these past two years, but today I reckon she might have a little in return.'

Jacob hoped that were true. He nodded and rounded the doorway, apprehension as to what might be said ruining the excitement that had been building every day for the last two years.

And then… There she was…

Alice sat on the hospital bed in a white summer frock that fell around her ankles. Her hair was tied back to reveal a slim neckline. She was almost gaunt from a two-year liquid diet that had given her exactly the nourishment she needed to stay healthy and alive but little sustenance. She had certainly lost a dress size or two. But where her body was frail, her sapphire-blue eyes still shone bright with bewitching power, and just like the last time Jacob had seen her sitting upright, they were filled with tears once more. She didn't speak just yet, she couldn't. Instead, she held out her arms and Jacob rushed to fill them with the kind of embrace one can only experience when your love returns from the dead. Both of them held on tightly to what was once lost and refused to let go in fear of reality kicking in, a reality where they were once again apart, and once again alone.

'I thought you were dead,' Alice cried while she peppered his brow and cheeks with kisses.

Jacob brought his hands up to cradle his wife's cheeks and

kissed her lips firmly. 'I am not so easily lost to this world, my beautiful Pebble, but I must confess, I am eager to hear about this journey you have endured in its entirety, as it sounds quite the caper indeed.'

'Baby, the nurses said you visited every day. I know it seems crazy, but whenever you were telling me about your day, it seemed to be shaping my dreams. The story in my head was almost mimicking the stories – at least, that's what my nurse has been telling me.'

Jacob smiled and sat next to his wife, taking her hand in his own. 'Had I known that, I might have tried to brainwash you.'

Jacob laughed and Alice punched him in the arm, causing him to hold it in mock pain.

'I'm serious, Jay. The nurses told me your stories. When you started to benefit from your therapy, I saw it happen. When the medication took its toll on you, I saw it happen. And when my mother...' Alice paused and closed her eyes for a heartbeat to try and find the strength to finish her statement.

'She had a stroke about 12 months ago,' Jacob explained. 'Strangely, it tied in almost to the day with you waking up from the induced coma and falling into that unresponsive state. We nearly lost her, and quite honestly we are lucky to have you both here with us today.'

Alice looked up and took in what Jacob was saying. Every word, no matter the grim nature of the subject, was a pleasure to hear. His absence had been hard, and his presence by her side was a joy she had felt she would never feel again.

'I wonder why I took the news of her falling so ill as a death in my world. What do you think my mind was trying to tell me?'

Jacob took a deep breath before he answered, struggling to find the words. 'I think your mind was confused, for the same month that your mum fell ill, I lost Grandma.'

Alice took her husband in her arms and pulled him close. 'Jay, I'm so sorry, I wasn't there, I didn't even... What happened?' She shuffled closer and held Jacob's arm tightly.

'She had struggled since losing both my gramps and then my

dad. I think she just stopped taking care of herself, and in the end that took its toll. It wasn't your fault, baby, far from it, but maybe the guilt of not being there for me manifested itself through your dreams.' Jacob sighed but looked into Alice's eyes with relief. 'I'm just glad you are back with us, Pebble; we have a lot to talk about.'

'That sounds ominous,' said Alice, yawning. The two years of sleep had taken their toll.

'I'll say no more until John and Angela get here.'

'John and Angela? I'm not sure I've ever heard you call them by name before. It's usually "your mum" and "your dad", and with no small amount of disdain, either.'

Alice was only half joking, although Jacob would have struggled to disagree. He had never bonded with them as Alice would have wanted – not until recently, anyway.

'Pebble, things have changed these past 18 months, and a lot of it has been for the better, but I must confess I have mixed feelings about how this might play out. So, can you do me a favour? I need you to know how much we all love you and how very proud you should be of us all.'

Alice almost couldn't believe what she was hearing. 'Us all? I have to say it's a pleasant surprise to hear you talk about my family like this. I guess I can take solace in the fact that some good has come from all this.'

NO

NO GOOD COMES FROM YOU BEING HERE

IT'S NOT REAL

8 May, one year before

'Ahab? A strange choice even for the most dedicated Herman Melville fan,' said Dr Phillips. 'Tell me, why name it after the captain and not the whale? After all, the whale would be apt, in terms of both scale and design.'

'Because the whale was just trying to go about its business,' said Jacob, 'trying to live its best life. Captain Ahab was the true monster. He was dedicating his whole existence to killing that whale, to sinking that whale and taking its life into the bleak void of the cold ocean floor. This thing inside of me is much more like that. It's the evil trying to harm the innocent.'

'Do you believe yourself an innocent party, Jacob?'

'I don't believe I'm guilty of the kind of crime that deserves the punishment I so often receive,' said Jacob defiantly.

'Then I'm glad to say, Mr Brooking, that we are getting somewhere.'

Chapter 4: In Darkness

Song of the day: 'The Soul Searchers' by Paul Weller

Winter 1994

Tankerton, Kent, UK

The dark was his protection. He couldn't see a thing, and that meant nothing could see him. But it was also his enemy, for the shadows were where the creature slept, where it plotted and where it watched. Hiding from monsters under his quilt was becoming a far-too-regular occurrence. For a boy of 14 years, Jacob had to admit that he felt a little childish. He had told his mother a few days before, but her attention always seemed elsewhere as she dealt with the demons of her own past.

'Just be brave, Jacob. You're a big boy now. You don't hear Samuel complaining of monsters hiding in the shadows, do you?'

'No, Mum, he doesn't.'

Marie Brooking lit another cigarette and ruffled his hair. She loved him, Jacob knew that, and he certainly had no right to complain about his upbringing, but he had always felt like he was the wrong piece in his mother's picture puzzle. Like she was disappointed he wasn't quite the child she had wanted him to be.

He had told his brother too, but Samuel had started to freak out at the thought of a creature in the room next door, leaving Jacob no choice but to pass the whole thing off as a joke.

So, he was here alone, as per usual. His exhalations were

trapped inside the confines of his safe house, and his breathing was becoming difficult. The quilt was tucked under his body so tightly that no limbs could reach for a hold on him. Jacob had pictured himself as a caterpillar getting ready for its transformation, a chrysalis of anxiety and panic. It had started when his father had turned the hall light off and closed his own bedroom door with a heavy thud. Jacob felt alone; in fact, today he had felt more alone than ever.

That morning

Jacob climbed into his dad's car and excitedly turned on the cassette player. His father's taste in music was, at least in Jacob's young eyes, second to none. A lover of soul and country rock, Paul Brooking inspired his son in more ways than he would ever know, but the first way he was to influence Jacob was with music.

The Electric Light Orchestra came on, much to the delight of Jacob, who quickly pulled on his seat belt as his father got in the car. The nearly new Peugeot 505 GTI was an amazing car to sit in, and he would admit to anyone who would listen that sitting by his father's side was his favourite place to be. The blue velour seats were warm and welcoming, and the sporty nature of the car seemed to hug him as his father went round corners with youthful abandon. His father had offered to drop him off at his friend's house. It wasn't a long walk there, but the rain that showered down on the cold December day would certainly have made it an unpleasant one.

'Did you read that article I left you out, son?'

'The West Ham United one? It doesn't make for great reading, but I think Harry is the right guy for us. I know you disagree, though.'

'It's not that I disagree, as I'm not sure there is anyone better out there right now in terms of leading us forward. There's just something about his car-salesman nature that rubs me the wrong way. Still, we should beat Charlton at home this weekend.'

The rest of the journey played out in silence. That wasn't uncommon for time spent with Paul Brooking, a man who didn't believe in conversation for the sake of it. When Paul said something, it always paid to listen.

The grey Peugeot rode the kerb gently as they arrived at Dinger's house. He wasn't a friend that Jacob's father particularly liked. Paul had accused him on more than one occasion of only hanging out at the Brooking house because Jacob had the better computer. No comment had been made today, though, with the play having been organised at Dinger's house for a change.

'Thanks, Pop,' said Jacob as he unbuckled his seat belt and leaned over to kiss his father on the cheek.

Much to his surprise, his dad pulled away and instead just tapped him on the leg with his open hand.

'Getting a little old for a kiss goodbye, son. You just go and have a good day.'

He doesn't love you anymore

'Oh, OK, Dad, sure, I'll see you at home later,' Jacob said in shock as he climbed out of the car and gently pressed the door closed.

He still kisses Samuel goodbye

Yeah, but Sam's younger, thought Jacob, trying his best to convince himself that this wasn't a personal thing. But it wasn't something that he was ever going to forget. Jacob had always wanted to be treated like a young man and not a kid. But now that time was here, he was frightened. He just couldn't shake the feeling that it was the first sign of his father giving up on him.

Paul Brooking, though, never gave that moment another thought, for Paul loved his son.

I can see you, said the creature, as Jacob felt the weight of its mass press down on his mattress.

I can smell you, said the creature, as it wrapped its long viscous tentacles around Jacob's cocoon.

I can taste you, said the creature, as it enveloped him in such a grip that Jacob thought he would surely be crushed.

They are right to bully you at school, the creature spat.

They are right to love you less than your brother

You are pathetic, and I taste only the weakness that drenches your skin as you cower from me, like a beaten dog, under the very cover of darkness that you know gives me strength

Jacob wasn't sure if the voice – or the creature that projected it, for that matter – was real, but he knew that the pain was real. He knew that he couldn't breathe and that he was starting to black out. Why it hated him Jacob didn't understand, and his hope that the other kids at school were tormented by monsters of their own had been misplaced – the few students who had been willing to talk to him about it had found no middle ground with him at all. It seemed he was alone in his relationship with the shadow leviathan, and as the weight of its mass started to crush him, and his ribs started to splinter and crack, he realised that actually he had very little in his life other than the creature's hate. His parents seemed to not even recognise his place in the family anymore. His brother had started calling him Gummy Bear, just like the kids at school, and what chance did he possibly have with that beautiful girl from the school next door? The last of his air escaped his lungs and his body started to convulse.

'Son, I'm here, little buddy,' said his dad, pulling the quilt from around Jacob's constricted body and holding him in place as he thrashed around like he was afflicted by some kind of demonic possession.

'Dad!' called Jacob. He reached forward with tear-stained cheeks and rasping lungs.

'I'm here, son, just breathe.' Paul pulled his son into his chest and kissed his brow. 'Where has all this come from? For weeks now I've seen you at war with yourself, and I can't for the life of me understand where all this angst is coming from.'

Jacob couldn't find the words to explain what he was going through. He felt broken, alone and like no one else would understand his pain. What could he say to his father now that would help him rationalise his conflict?

'It was just a bad dream,' said Jacob, trying to regain some composure. 'I couldn't even tell you what it was about.'

'OK, son. Just know that I'm only next door, OK?'

'Yeah, alright, Dad, thanks.'

Jacob's father left the room and left the door ajar, just enough for the hall light to shine on his son's face. Leaving the landing light on may have seemed like a small gesture to others, but to Jacob it meant the world.

Chapter 5: Ruby Slippers

Song of the day: 'The Rip'
by Portishead

Summer 2009

St Martin's Hospital, Canterbury, Kent, UK

'Are you ready to talk about her?' said Dr Phillips with an air of caution in her voice.

'Evan? I hope that bitch rots in hell.'

Dr Phillips seemed hurt by Alice's words, a reaction not missed by Alice.

'No, Alice, not Evan, but at least we've established that you're not ready to talk about that part of your life yet. I meant your mother. It must be an amazing feeling to know your mother is alive. How does that feel?'

'Oh… Honestly, it doesn't feel real that either of them is still here. Jacob or my mum. It's a dream to me, and my mind won't allow it to take root – not until I can see, touch or hear them, I guess.'

'Well, they shall be here soon enough. I hear Jacob was already on his way to see you when he got the call, and your parents are close behind.'

'Jacob and my dad in the same room, and I'm too weak to run away – please, Doc, put me back to sleep.'

Doctor and patient shared an awkward laugh that turned into an even more awkward silence – one that was broken in the most unexpected way.

'You might find this hard to believe, but your father has a new-found respect for Jacob,' said the doctor.

'I'll believe that when I see it,' said Alice.

'Remember these words,' said Dr Phillips, 'if you remember nothing else that I tell you. It's OK that things have changed in your absence. You might even be pleasantly surprised.'

Two hours later

Angela Petalow wrapped her arms tightly around a daughter whom she had thought was lost to another world. Tears of joy and disbelief ran down her cheeks as an overwhelmed Alice held her with equal vigour and love. They refused to break the embrace, and they couldn't find the words to form coherent sentences. 'I love you' was all that could be heard escaping from both sets of lips in between the crying and smattering of long-missed kisses. But the joy and relief they felt was radiating off of them in such abundance that Jacob felt warmth just to be in the presence of such love.

'I never thought I would see you again,' said Alice, kissing her mother squarely on the lips.

'All that matters is that you are here with us now, because we have so longed for this day.' Angela turned and placed a cupped hand on Jacob's face. 'Isn't that right, my favourite son?'

Alice was so overwhelmed with joy that she didn't allow the shock of such an unusually sweet moment between her mother and husband to break into her thought process.

'That's right, Mum, this day has been long overdue,' said Jacob, caressing his mother-in-law's hand in return.

'Oh my god, what has been going on between you lot while I've been away?' said Alice. 'I feel like I've woken up in the twilight zone.'

Angela took her daughter's hands and sat next to her on the edge of the bed, feeling an instant contentment, one that she never thought she would feel again. 'In times of hardship, sometimes the smallest things can bring us all together.'

Alice furrowed her brow. 'What on earth are you talking about? I'm not sure me being asleep for two years would qualify as a "small thing". Actually, speaking of things that are far from small, where's Dad?'

'Well, I guess I would be here.' The deep and brooding voice of her father split a path between Angela and Jacob like he was parting the Red Sea. His huge frame filled the doorway with its unnatural width and height, and his demeanour was stern and unmoving, as always. John Petalow was a man mountain and a colossus, one who had always hated her husband for never being "quite enough" for his Alice, and yet she could see something different in him, something kind and protective. Where once he had been a bull, now he carried the air of a giant stag – majestic and family orientated, despite its strength and indifference towards others outside of the herd. 'I was parking the car, love. I dropped your mother off at the entrance because she couldn't wait to see you.' He took a few strides into the room with his arms still folded and kissed Alice square on the forehead. 'Welcome home, monkey.'

It was unusual to hear so many words from her father, even under such a unique situation, but Alice knew that he was happy to see her back on her feet – well, at least sitting upright.

'And this, my son, I believe to be yours.' John Petalow unravelled what Alice had assumed was a defensive crossed-arm gesture and passed the most beautiful auburn-haired child to Jacob.

This isn't real

'Jacob, what's going on?' said Alice as her heart rate grew in both speed and aggression.

The silent child smiled at Jacob while holding onto his tie as if for dear life.

'Alice Marie Brooking, I present to you your daughter, Dorothy Gale Brooking.'

LIES LIES LIES LIES

As Jacob turned her in Alice's direction, Dorothy pushed away from the mother she had only ever experienced as asleep or in a trance-like state. The flame-haired princess had never known her mum, and all the knowledge she had of her was from the stories her dad would tell her each night. Alice was struggling to figure out what was happening – what had happened – and her confusion threatened to send her back into the false reality she had just come from. Alice reached out tenderly to hold the shrinking child's hand but fell short as a young Dorothy cowered from a touch she had never known, leaving Alice to fall forward and into an abyss she, once again, couldn't have seen coming.

Chapter 6: The Infant and the Abyss

Song of the day: 'Hero'
by Regina Spektor

Summer 2009

St Martin's Hospital, Canterbury, Kent, UK

Alice had fallen like this before, after the assault by Thomas many years before, but where on that occasion she had blacked out and woken up on the carpet of her childhood home, this time she hit the ground hard, and the jolt through her body shook her to her bones as she rapidly decelerated to a standstill. A foot of water had broken her fall, enough to stop serious injury, but the air was knocked from her in one huge and forced exhale that left her gasping.

'Alice!'

She could hear William's voice calling her, and yet as she rose to her feet to check her surroundings, only two things embraced her – darkness, and the murky ocean that rose up to her knee.

'Alice! Come back to me.'

William's voice was coming at her from every angle and she felt her equilibrium tested as she took to her feet in the abyss of pure midnight. Alice spun around on a floor so black it possibly didn't exist and looked for the source of the call, but to no avail. Her movements caused ripples in the water, which looked more like oil, and this brought movement to her attention. Things were swimming about her ankles within the dark liquid. Obsidian tentacles whipped about in a frenzy, making it look like the ground beneath her was actually alive. This couldn't be real... *Could it?* Remembering back to a session with Dr Phillips, Alice clenched her fists tightly and closed her eyes. She focused only on her physical self and released the tension slowly from her fists, before opening her eyes once more.

There sat in front of her was the image from the hospital ward. She was lying on the bed, catatonic and oblivious to her apparent daughter pointing at her motionless body. Alice was watching it play out as if on a screen. She could see her mum rushing around, screaming for nurses to come and help, while her father just placed a reassuring hand on her shoulder. Jacob, with Dorothy held tight in his arms, looked like the father she knew he would be. His eyes were locked on hers, and she could see him mouthing the words, 'You've got this, Pebble, we believe in you.'

'Alice!'

Alice shot round and looked behind, to see herself seemingly unconscious once more, this time on the soft tartan rug of the picnic that William had set up. His hands pressed tightly on her motionless heart, as he knelt by her side. But this was different, because William was looking straight at her, not at the image of her motionless corpse in front of her.

'It's not real, Alice, come back to me.'

'William, I can't move,' said Alice as she met him in conversation for the first time in the surrealness of the abyss.

'Baby, you have to try. It's not real, any of it,' William shouted, trying to stay strong, just in case Alice needed to use his voice as an anchor.

'What's not real, William?'

Then, as though afraid of something he could see behind Alice, he scrambled to his feet, falling backwards as he hurried.

'NO!' he screamed. 'It can't be real.'

Alice turned to find the vision of her family replaced by her mirrored demon self.

Hello child

It wore the same white frock as Alice and yet the frock was stained and filthy. This creature of broken skin and missing teeth was grinning, its over-sized fangs the only thing on the apparition that were not rotten with decay. Once again, Alice was frozen still. The creature, with limbs of unnatural length, stepped forward to grip Alice by her arms. The creature's bony fingers, each ended with black, razor-sharp talons, pierced her flesh as it spoke in its wicked and broken tongue.

IT'S NOT REAL, CHILD

Alice fell into panic. The stench of the creature's breath was almost overwhelming. Alice clenched her fists and closed her eyes once more. Ignoring the pain in her arm and the hot acrid breath of the oppressor, a feat that wasn't easy as she felt her blood trickle down her wrists, she slowly unclenched her hands and opened her eyes with a bellowing shriek to find her hand holding a tiny ruby shoe, and as she looked up, once more in the real world of the hospital ward, she was faced with a confused Dorothy, a young lady almost amused at the audacity of this new woman in her life, who had stolen her shoe.

'Dorothy,' Alice whispered.

'Dorothy,' Jacob replied reassuringly.

Dorothy said nothing, while pointing at her father with a smile.

Alice watched Dorothy giggle as she reached up to Jacob's face, letting the bristles of his short, well-kept beard tickle her hand. Alice herself tried to hold it together, knowing, without any doubt, where that scar on her belly had come from.

Chapter 7: Country Roads

Song of the day: 'All I Need'
by Air

Summer 2009

Faversham, Kent, UK

It had been a week since Alice had woken from her nightmare, and yet she felt more out of place in the waking world than she ever had before. She was sure that this was real, but that didn't mean she had wanted it to be so. She sat in the passenger seat of Jacob's Mercedes and watched the beautiful green countryside of Kent zip past at speed. She was unsure how to feel just yet. Everyone kept telling her how happy she should be for having finally woken up, which would have been fine had she had any recollection of being asleep, yet what had actually happened was that the snow globe of her life had been shaken with such vigour that nothing really made sense anymore. She had an 18-month-old child whom she had no recollection of even carrying. She had a husband and a mother back from beyond the grave and a boyfriend who in reality was not her boyfriend and had no idea what the daft young coma victim was talking about. None of it made sense. She had tried to write it all down with Doctor Phillips, and, on paper at least, it all tied in. William, her boyfriend in the dream world, looked like Dr Williams in the real world. She had imagined her mothers death when Jacob had sat by her side one night and spoken of Angela having a minor stroke. It all added up – even the day that Dorothy would have been conceived fell into place. Alice couldn't fathom how she had never noticed a bump of any kind, although she did remember the struggle of getting into her dress on that awful day of mirror shards and Jacob's return. One thing still didn't click, though: why she would imagine Jacob's death and his eventual release from her life.

'Jay, tell me again about the news you gave me this year – you know, when you used to sit by my bedside.'

Jacob took a while to answer. 'Well, I told you about your mum, and about the shop that I saw for sale – the one I thought would make a great studio for you.' Jacob fidgeted with obvious unease as he continued to reel off things that were not of any help to Alice. 'And then I told you that, erm, that I'd met someone.'

Alice felt weak. She was confused and heartbroken at the news that she could never have seen coming, even though there was no reason for it not to have been a possibility.

'Then why are you here, Jacob, if you have met someone else? Or am I missing something? Why don't you help me to connect these dots?' Alice was glad that her supposed daughter was in her father's Range Rover just ahead.

'Because you are my wife, Alice, and despite the fact we broke up – and you cannot deny that we did – it doesn't mean I stopped loving you or even wanting you back.' Jacob sighed deeply and took a moment to find the right line of defence. 'I came back to you that day in San Diego because I wanted to make things right with you. I'd had extensive therapy and had come a million miles from the person who had left you those three months before, but I never planned to find you cutting your own throat open, I never planned for you to go to sleep for two years, and I certainly never planned to meet anyone, even though I had no idea if you would ever wake up.' Jacob tried to take Alice's hand but was quickly rejected. 'Alice, I never thought you were going to wake up, and yet I still came and sat with you each day in the blind hope that you would.'

The Mercedes pulled into the Petalows' driveway. John was carrying a fast-asleep Dorothy into the house.

'I'll get the bags out,' said Jacob. 'Do you need a hand getting to your room, love?'

Alice scowled and reached for the door, but Jacob stopped her with a firm grip on her arm.

'Alice, I've done nothing wrong here.'

Alice sat back once again. 'Then you won't mind telling me everything, will you?'

Everything? Well, this is going to be fun, said Ahab.

Yes, old friend, you might want to stay out of this one, thought Jacob.

Chapter 8: The Dry Roast

Song of the day: 'She's Crazy'
by JT Coldfire

Autumn 2008

Faversham, Kent, UK

'Double espresso, Mr Brooking?' said the barista at Barton Millie's Coffee Cup, one of those modern types of coffee house where the staff all had tattoos and suede aprons.

'Yes please, Jessica, and would you be so kind as to run it over to my table with a smoked cheese croissant?'

Jacob handed over a crisp ten-pound note from his money clip and refused the change with a wave of his hand. His morning had been productive. He had worn his best navy suit and tie to try to show the other shareholders at the Gallantry that he was still in charge of the operation despite having to sell 30% of the restaurant to cover Alice's medical bills. He needn't have bothered, as he had methodically picked the shareholders – Canterbury's best offerings of poor little rich kids who just wanted to own a share in a fancy restaurant – so as to ensure they would always feel subservient to him.

He sat at the small table that he frequented most days and laid out his newspaper, pondering for a moment just when exactly he had become so calculated. Still, it seemed to be working for him, as business was on the up: his take from the business seemed to have enjoyed a slight growth, despite his drop in shares and a reduction of time spent in the kitchen. He still wrote the menus and tasted the dishes, and a random fiery tirade at a slack member of staff always kept the crew on their toes, but mostly his days were filled with Dorothy giggling to herself and him marvelling at how such a broken man could create such a happy and perfect thing. Dotty wasn't here today, as he had work to do; she would be sitting in the garden with her gramps. John Petalow had softened since her entry into the world eight months earlier, and the giant of a man would sit and play with her for hours, while Angela would tend to the various wild flowers that filled the Petalows' five-acre garden.

With work out of the way, it was Jacob's time to breathe. Being a single father had come to Jacob with ease; it was the only thing he had found easy in all his years alive. Keeping her happy and safe had given him a focus he had never experienced before. It was all about her, no one else. Dorothy Gale Brooking and her beautiful smile had killed his selfishness in just a few months, and the bond they shared had proved to him that it was possible to love someone so much that it fixes you on every level.

Jacob Brooking had never felt so normal, and it was a good place to be. He would still hear the monster in his thoughts, from time to time – that was normal. As Jessica brought him his coffee and croissant, he noticed her blush, and yet the voice mocked him, tried to bring him low once more.

She thinks you're a loner

Well, she wouldn't be wrong. Jacob smiled, fully aware that friends were not really his forte.

And old, the voice cackled.

Well, that's just rude. Let's not forget that you are the same age as me, you old bastard.

Jacob had developed a better way of dealing with his inner voice of late. Dr Phillips had told him that if he couldn't win the fight with his inner demon, he should stop fighting it.

'Thank you, Jessica. How's that boyfriend of yours? Still keeping you happy, love?'

'You know how it is, Mr Brooking. Until he pulls his finger out, I'll always be on the lookout for something better.' Jessica turned to hide her blush and gave an obvious wiggle to draw his attention down.

'Really, Jay, you will flirt with anyone, but do you have to tease "the help" with your endless charms?'

Jacob looked up and nearly choked on the first bite of his pastry.

'Oh my god – Evan. I don't know what to say. I...'

Well, you're fucked.

'Don't panic, Jay, just bloody give me a hug so we can kill this awkwardness.'

Evan opened her arms up to Jacob, which did nothing to ease his fear, but he surprised himself and stood to embrace her all the same.

'Of course. I'm sorry, Evan. How are you?'

'I'm really well, thanks. May I join you?'

Evan motioned at the seat opposite and then pulled herself into the spot. Skinny jeans so tight they were almost painted onto her perfectly curved rear drew Jacob's attention with little effort, despite the crippling fear in his heart.

Evan sighed. 'I must confess, I had kind of hoped you would look worse than you do, Jay.'

Jacob tried to force his grin to look natural, but failed. 'From you I take that as a compliment. Evan, listen, I need to say...'

Evan cut him off quickly. 'I'm sorry too, but I don't think us bringing up the past is how we enjoy this impromptu coffee, do you?'

Jacob relaxed slightly and drew in his puffed-out chest. 'I am sorry, though, I need you to know that. I'm not that guy anymore.'

Evan reached over the table and placed a reassuring hand on his. 'Jacob Brooking, I'm not made of glass, OK? And if the rumours are to be believed, I hear you have had a harder few years than I.'

She knows

'I didn't know my news had spread so quickly and was so important to the community in general?'

Evan smiled softly and seemed genuine as she squeezed his hand ever so slightly before releasing it. 'Jay, your wife tried to kill herself and then gave birth to your child whilst in a coma – a coma it seems she might be in for the rest of her life. Do you think that's not gossip-worthy, especially when we share a lot of the same friends still?'

Jacob laughed.

'OK, they may be employees to you,' said Evan, 'but they are friends to me, you big meanie managing director you.'

Evan parted her plump lips to reveal her perfect white teeth and a smile that had always had a power over him, much like her long blonde hair, which today was straightened and fell over her shoulders and past her breasts, almost to her lap.

'You look good, Evan. You always did. Can I get you a coffee whilst we catch up?' Jacob rose, knowing the answer already.

'A flat white please, Jay, and then you can tell me all about it.'

Jacob looked confused. 'All about what?'

Evan leaned forward, rested her elbow on the coffee table and gently cradled her jaw while twirling her hair between her fingers. 'About San Diego, Jacob. About what happened when you left me.'

Chapter 9: So, It's Gonna Be Forever?

Song of the day: 'Whiskey And You'
by Chris Stapleton

Summer 2009

Canterbury, Kent, UK

'Jacob, how could you?' Alice felt an overwhelming desire to scream, but the medication was doing its job of keeping her calm, at least on the surface.

'We broke up,' said Jacob. 'I went away for three months, and we haven't spoken a single word to each other in two years. I never thought you would wake up. I thought my life was just me and Dotty, and I bumped into her randomly. Would it make a difference if it was anyone else?'

For once, Jacob didn't sound like he was making excuses. His life hadn't stopped for two years, and he wasn't going to apologise for any choices he had made while struggling on his own.

'Well, I wonder if my parents would love you so much if they knew?' said Alice, sounding a little spoiled and hurt.

'They already know. I asked your mother's advice before I moved forward. How could I not? They have helped me raise our child, I had to show them that respect.'

Alice turned her gaze from him. 'Respect, Jay? What about respect for me? How about anyone in the world except for her?'

Dorothy let out a cry that immediately brought Jacob over to the mock playpen he had built for her out of cushions stolen from the couch.

'What's up, little boo?' said Jacob as he picked up his terrified daughter from the floor. 'Tell me.'

Dorothy clung to Jacob like he was about to vanish. Jacob went and sat next to Alice and tried to offer Dorothy over, but she wrapped her arms around her dad's body all the tighter.

'She hates me, Jay. That's why she doesn't want anything to do with me.'

'She will come around. This is all new to her. She hadn't heard you talk until last week, and now she's listening to you shout at me.' Jacob knew he had made a mistake with that last comment and so quickly tried to deflate the situation by waving Dorothy's hand at her angry mother.

'Don't you dare use this little club you two have going on to deflect what you have done, Jay. Not her – not Evan.'

Alice's voice was in check, knowing that scaring Dorothy was probably not the best way into her heart, but Jacob knew that he didn't have much choice other than to agree with Alice on this.

'You're right,' he said. 'I should have been more thoughtful. Together or apart, I owed you that, Alice. I was lonely, and knowing you had started dating so quickly after I had left on that godforsaken voyage… Well, I didn't think.'

Alice looked up at Jacob, confused. 'How do you know I was dating, when you were apparently lost at sea?'

'Because when I held you in my arms, blood pouring from the gaps in the compress I was forcing onto your neck wound, your date turned up to ask why you hadn't showed up to meet him at the Harbour Café. He walked in and attacked me, thinking it was me who had hurt you, but I wouldn't put you down. He eventually guided the paramedics into you from the road.' Jacob's voice trembled as he thought back to that day once more. 'Pebble, you can believe what you want, but I have not sat idle since that day, none of us have, and I'm sorry but I was struggling at the end to do it alone.'

Autumn 2008
Ten months earlier

Song of the day: 'Windows Are Rolled Down' by Amos Lee

'Jacob, hi, it's Evan. I know you have a lot going on, what with the baby and looking after Alice and all. I just wondered if I could lighten the load a little and make you dinner this week. Let you be you for a night. It doesn't have to mean anything.'

Do it, we like Evan

'Evan, I don't know what to say. That's so kind of you to offer, and certainly it's unexpected. Let me see if I can find a sitter for the night. I'll get back to you soon as.'

You're not even going to try, are you, coward?

'Great,' said Evan. 'I'm excited for you to see the new place, and I expect you to bring the wine – your taste is too expensive for my purse.'

You won't go. I'm not sure you deserve a girl that attractive

'Too expensive for your purse? Evan, your purse is a £1,500 Prada job. I know that because I bought the bastard thing.'

You don't have the backbone to follow through with this

'Yeah, but you didn't fill it with money, my darling Jacob. Right, I'll let you get back to whatever you were doing – or whomever, should I say.'

That was an attack, you know it was

Jacob held up the full diaper that he had been trying to change while speaking to Evan with the phone pressed between his shoulder and ear. 'Trust me when I say this, I would swap whatever it is you are doing with the task I'm handling right now.'

'All the more reason to get back to me with a positive answer, then. Goodbye, Mr Brooking, text me when you get the chance.'

'I'm on it. Give me an hour or two.'

Jacob put the phone down. He could barely hear his own thoughts due to Dorothy screaming at his poor attempt to replace her nappy, and all the chatter the voice in his head was throwing

37

his way.

I'm going to bloody go, he thought, I need a break.

What you need and what you deserve are two different things. She will probably slit her throat when you walk through the door, just like Alice di..

JUST LIKE ALICE DID? Is that what you were going to say? Because I'm tired of that broken record. I'm going because I want to go, and nothing you say will stop me. Jacob could hear himself shouting, even though the conversation was in his thoughts.

With that, the creature went silent, and then it smiled a smile that exposed every fanged tooth in its kraken-like beak.

Yes, Jacob, you are going to do exactly what you want to do. All this is on you, it always was

This time, the creature whispered, and its smile remained long after the sun had set.

Summer 2009

Canterbury, Kent, UK

Song of the day: 'Wait Up for Me' by Amos Lee

'So, this is it, then?' said Alice, defeated not only by the news, but by Jacob's honest account of it. 'We are not going to work this through and sort our marriage out?'

'I'm not saying anything other than this. You have come back into a world that has kept turning in your absence. We need to get you fit and healthy, Dorothy needs you to adapt into the mother that I know you are going to be, and you need to find yourself once more. I'll speak with Evan, but you must know that this, all of this, is all about you getting well, not us getting back together.'

Jacob stood up and held Dorothy out so her mother could kiss her brow.

'Goodnight, my angel,' Alice whispered.

Dorothy once again shied away into Jacob's arms.

'Goodbye, Pebble. Call me if you need me for anything.'

Before he could reach the door, Alice said his name.

'Thank you for being honest with me,' she said. 'I don't like what you have told me, in actual fact I hate it, but you never would have been this honest before, so I guess you have changed.'

Jacob smiled, gave a slight nod and pulled the door behind him.

Hours passed and Alice didn't move. *Why her*? was all she could keep asking herself. *Why Evan fucking Laurie?*

BECAUSE IT'S NOT REAL. COME BACK TO US, ALICE. IT'S NEVER BEEN REAL

The voice took Alice by surprise, for she had made a point of asking her father to remove all the mirrors from the house, and it was so very rare to hear it speak without a reflection. In fact, the only time she had ever heard the voice speak that clearly without a reflection had been at her mother's funeral, in the world that apparently wasn't real...

Alice snapped, and the tears of confusion that she had shed so many times these past few days returned with a vengeance. 'Where am I?' she sobbed, digging her nails once more into the soft flesh of her thigh.

Chapter 10: The Tell-Tale Heart

Song of the day: 'Damn Your Eyes' by Luce Dufault

Autumn 2008

Faversham, Kent, UK

As I take a seat upon this magnificent leather sofa, a sofa of deep stitches and brass finishing, the one that I have admired for so many years, it saddens my heart once more that I didn't have the courage to talk to you about this before, without, that is, having to pay for an hour of your time.

True! I'm negligent, very, very dreadfully negligent. I had been and am always such; I make as little time for you as you do for me, but why will you say that I am in love? The adoration I may have for this man has sharpened my senses, not taken them on flights of fantasy, not dulled them with words that you and I both know have little meaning in this real world, this painfully dreadful world. I know my senses are acute. I know my own mind. I have seen all things in the heaven and in the earth. I heard many things in hell and have come close to living them at times. I KNOW THIS WORLD! How, then, could I be in love? For to be in love, one must not be of this realm. Take my candour, please, and observe how healthily and how calmly I can tell you the whole story.

It is impossible to say how first the idea entered my brain; but once conceived, it haunted me day and night. I lusted for the man whose affections I had previously won. He had never wanted me the same. But he had never given me insult; even in the days before he left, he had begged forgiveness. For his gold I had no desire, although it certainly had its charms, and he had given it freely. Yet the idea came to me that he was more than just a flight of fancy out of nowhere. I think, in the end, it was his eyes! Yes, it was this! He had the eyes of an avenging angel, a viridian green, with a crystal pupil that refracted light as if not meant to give true reflection of such a wondrous creature. Whenever it fell upon me, my blood ran hot and my pulse rose in both tempo and depth; and so by degrees – very gradually – I made up my mind to take the heart of the man once more, and thus rid myself of the powerless longing forever. Not because I loved him... Because I didn't want to be so powerless to a man I was getting no return from.

Now this is the point. You fancy me in love. You, a woman of culture and class. A woman of higher education than most can dream of. Women in love know nothing. But you should have seen me. You should have seen how wisely I proceeded – with what caution, with what foresight, with what dissimulation I went to work! Does that sound like the madness of love? He never knew that my new place of work – another restaurant – was opposite his regular coffee shop, a chance that fate had thrown at us both. Fate... another made-up word for an irrational concept. I was never more taken by the man than during the whole week before I came to you today. And every morning, about midday, I pulled the silk rope of our blinds and opened them – oh so gently! The restaurant was so dark that no light shone out, yet enough was let in for me to see him each day. Oh, you would have laughed to see how unknowingly I had let him into my life! I undid the blind just so much that a single thin ray fell upon my vulture's eye. And this I did for seven long days, every morning at midday, but I found my eye impossible to close; and so it was impossible to do the work; for it was not the man who vexed me, but his power that held me so, unbeknownst to him. And every morning, when the day broke, I went boldly into the window bay and spoke courageously to him, calling him by name in a hearty tone, and inquiring how he had passed the night. Yet I would have to stop when the others came near, lest they think me mad. So, you see he would have been a very profound man, indeed, to suspect that every day, just at twelve, I looked in upon him while he sat by the window and drank his elixir of caffeine and dark magic.

Upon the eighth day, just yesterday in fact, I was less than my usually cautious self, a whimsy caused by lack of sleep from an unrelated matter of mind, and in letting in the light, a rare mistake was made. A watch's minute hand moves more quickly than did mine and I lost a quarter of an hour to his gaze. Never before that day had I felt my powers so greatly diminished. I could scarcely contain my feelings of loneliness since the last sight I had of the man, whom you laughably say I must love. To think that there I was, opening the blinds once more, little by little, and he not even to dream of my secret deeds or thoughts. I fairly restrained a chuckle at the idea; and perhaps he saw me, knew I was there; for he moved once more to the table I forever saw him at, as if he knew no other table would provide me with ample view. *He knows*, I told myself, for why else would he always sit there? Now you may think that I drew back, but no. My room was as dark as the cobbled streets were light, and with the veil of darkness, the veil that protected me each and every day, doing the job that I had called on it to do, I watched once more, and so I knew that he could not see the opening of the blinds. I kept quite still and said nothing. For a whole minute that felt akin to an hour I did not move a muscle, and he could not see me. I did not catch acknowledgement in his eyes of green, jade and emerald – yes, emerald. He was still listening to music, an earphone in one ear and one hanging loosely about his neck, just in case a pretty little waitress chose to talk to him. But they could only dream of such a man; just as I have done, night after night, thinking of the man and his lips upon my flesh. And yet you say I am in love. Does my clarity of thought stand for nothing? I care little for your fantasy and the use of words better left in the poetry books of forgotten scholars.

When I had waited a long time – minutes? Hours? Days perhaps? – but very patiently, without seeing him change position, I resolved to open a very, very little crevice in the window itself. So as to maybe breathe a little of the same air that he himself had taken into the very lungs I so desired would breathe their warmth over my shoulder once more. So, I opened it, you cannot imagine how stealthily, until, at length, a bright sunray, like the thread of a spider, shot from out the crevice and fell full upon my vulture's eye. The window was open, it was open wide, and I grew scared as I saw him look in my direction. But I could see nothing to tell me of the crime being caught. The man's face or demeanour remained unbothered, a stroke of luck, as I had directed the ray, as if by instinct, precisely upon the damned spot where I stood watching. He sipped at his elixir and mouthed the words of such a song that I could not imagine. I was fully aware of my actions and of his, and have I not told you that what you mistake for love is but over-acuteness of the senses?

Now, I say, there came to my ears a low, dull, quick sound, such as a watch makes when enveloped in cotton. I knew that sound well, too. It was the beating of my heart. It increased my longing, as the beating of a drum stimulates the soldier into courage.

So I was exposed to him, but even then I kept still. I scarcely breathed. I held the blind motionless. I tried to see how steadily I could maintain the ray upon the form. I understood I was exposed and yet felt thrilled within my own form. Meantime the hellish tattoo of my heart increased. It grew quicker and quicker, and louder and louder, every instant. Mark me well, for I have told you that I am nervous: so, I am. And so I was at the hour of twelve, before our patrons joined us for lunches, drinks, the clamour of false lives and wishes unfulfilled. But amid the dreadful silence of that empty restaurant, so strange a noise as my own heartbeat excited me to near uncontrollable terror. Yet, for some minutes longer I refrained and stood still. The beating grew louder, louder! I thought my heart must burst, and now a new anxiety seized me – the sound would be heard by a customer or member of my crew. The hour had come for me to focus my attention elsewhere! And with a loud yell of frustration, I threw open the front doors and leapt into the cobbled streets, quickly pulling down the awnings to protect our al fresco diners from the very rays that had exposed my eye. Moving quickly and in open secrecy as I kept my back to the man, through fear that he might recognise me once more, in an instant I dragged my menu board to its home upon the floor and pulled the heavy wooden slats into position. I then smiled gaily, to find the deed so far done. But, for many minutes, as I retreated back within the sanctuary of the dark, the heart beat on with a muffled sound. This, however, did not vex me; it would not be heard through my blouse, not by kin nor patron alike. At length it ceased. The feeling dead until tomorrow. I placed my hand upon my heart and held it there many minutes. There was no pulsation that felt abnormal. The rush that the man had pulled upon me had subsided, as it did each day. His emerald eyes would trouble me no more.

If still you think me in love, you will think so no longer when I describe the wise precautions I took for the concealment of my emotions. As the bell sounded upon the hour, there came a holler at the street door. I went down to greet it with a light heart, for what had I now to fear? There entered three handsome men, who introduced themselves, with perfect suavity, as men of the local law firm. They were led to a table with a view of the beautiful town that surrounded them. Their drinks order was taken with jollity and efficiency, for what had I to fear? I bade the gentlemen a good lunch and a good stay.

The men were satisfied. My manner had convinced them. I was singularly at ease. They sat, and they ate in silence before they drank and enjoyed a little hubris, whilst the talk of success and women's hearts won dominated the air about them, and whilst I answered cheerily to any question thrown my way. I was pleasant and open as I always am and have been, for they chatted of familiar things. But, ere long, I felt myself getting pale and wished them gone. My head ached and my heart more so, and I fancied a ringing in my ears; but still they sat and still chatted. The ringing became more distinct. It continued and became more acute. I talked more freely to get rid of the feeling, forgetting my place as host; but it continued and gained definiteness, until, with certainty, I found that I had to make my excuses and return to the safety of the cellar.

My heart once more pounded within my chest and I found myself short of breath. A young server joined me, of young years and fair face, no knowledge of the world yet imparted on her soul. Although not seeking safety like I, she proudly proclaimed, 'Miss Evan, the table by the window, the table of money and of arrogance, they ask for you, Miss Evan, they clamour for your time once more.'

I waved the young cherub away with a gesture of indifference. Why would they not be gone? I paced the floor with heavy strides, as if frustrated by the desires of the men, when it was the desires of one man I wanted and nothing more. Oh God! What could I do? I rallied my thoughts and I took to my task.

'Gentlemen, what shall it be?' I asked with the mime of someone who might actually enjoy that damned profession. But I heard nothing over my own racing heart, as I looked up through the window to see him leave, the man who took my breath from me with nothing but his presence. My heart now throbbed, and I feared all would hear it. It grew louder, louder and louder still! And yet the men chatted pleasantly and smiled as if ignorant to my plight. Was it possible they heard not? Almighty God! No, no! They heard! They knew! They were making a mockery of my torment! This I thought, and this I think. But anything was better than this agony! Anything was more tolerable than this derision! I could bear those hypocritical smiles no longer! I felt that I must scream or die! And now, again! It grows louder, louder, louder, louder!

'Gentlemen, but a moment, please.'

I opened the front door to find the sun, the air and the cobbles of the street, but he was gone, and with that, also the beating of my heart. Only emptiness remained, and the hollow shell of the cold woman you raised took herself aside to devalue the incident as nothing more than tiredness.

So, you may say I am in love, but really, do I sound of such a fantastical mindset? When I remember everything so calculatedly and without whimsical nostalgia, does that really tell you of love, mother?

Chapter 11: The Coward and the Bear

Song of the day: 'Porcelain Gods' by Paul Weller

Autumn 2005

Camber, East Sussex, UK

There was a thunderous knock at the door.

'Come in,' Jacob shouted with gay abandon. He didn't have much time, and his blasted tie wasn't falling right at all, but he was doing his best to look presentable on his wedding day. Of all days, surely this was the one on which his tie must hang impeccably. Jacob looked over his shoulder to see the hulking figure of Alice's father squeezing into the small room, much like a rhino trying to turn around in an elevator. His father-in-law was an intimidating man to everyone. Even the muscular frame of Jacob seemed quite pathetic compared to the behemoth that was John Petalow, and it wasn't even muscle that made the man so big; he was just huge, his arms like tree trunks and his barrelled body like a samurai's suit of armour. It was Jacob's hotel, but even he would have been hard-pressed to take the much larger bridal suite off his fiancée, so they would have to dance around each other here.

'What can I do for you, John? I must confess, I'm a little pressed for time,' Jacob said as he turned back to the mirror.

Don't turn your back on him, you fool, said the voice in a shrill and almost surprised voice.

In the next few minutes, Jacob would realise two things: firstly, that his years of training at the gym and playing rugby for Canterbury meant absolutely nothing when it came down to life and death; and, secondly, that the monster in his head didn't always lie to get him into trouble.

John Petalow's hands were like shovels, and as he gripped Jacob's neck from behind, much like an adult lion might carry a newborn cub, there was nothing Jacob could do to escape. His face was smashed up against the mirror in front of him, causing a crack that ran from top to bottom. Jacob tried to speak out in protest at the violence being forced on him, but his oppressor's massive hand was restraining his airway to the point that nothing but a whimper was escaping his throat.

'Son, of all the things I am known for, after breaking necks, the thing I am known for most is never forgetting, and I remember saying to you many years ago, when you sat in front of me, begging, like a dog, to take my Alice from me, I said, "If you're talking, then you are not listening, and right now I need you to listen." I remember those words clearly.' John Petalow leaned in close to Jacob's ear and, in a low growl, said, 'Jacob, do you remember those words? Nod once if you do, OK?'

Jacob felt his head nod once as John's hand shook him like a rag doll.

'Good. Now the same rules apply. So when I let go, you are not going to speak, because I need you to listen. Nod again if you comprehend what I'm saying.'

Jacob once again felt the involuntary shake of his neck result in the most basic of nods, and then he felt himself released. He crashed down to one knee and drew breath like never before, although he showed enough resolve to stand and face John, knowing better than to say anything. He gritted his teeth and prepared for the bullshit "if you ever hurt my daughter" speech that he was certain was coming.

He was wrong. And the next few words out of John's mouth knocked the colour out of Jacob's tanned skin and the broadness out of his shoulders.

'I know about you and Evan Laurie. You were seen by my

delivery driver, at the crack of dawn the other day. He had ten kilos of Scottish salmon for you that he couldn't get a signature for. Why? Well, I'm glad you asked. It was because when he went to find you, you had that restaurant manager of yours bent over your desk. Tell me, Jacob, am I missing anything so far? Nope? Then I shall carry on.'

As he spoke, John never took his eyes off Jacob's, and Jacob felt smaller with every second that the gaze fell over him.

'You had the fucking cheek to ring me a few hours later, to tell me, ME, just how disappointed you were that my delivery drivers have stopped bothering to ask for a signature when they leave their invoice. "It's just bloody lazy" were your words. The thing is, that delivery driver wouldn't have said a word to me had I not called him into the office to reprimand him on your behalf. Does that taste good, Jacob? Because I hope you choke on that fucking irony.'

John finally turned his back on Jacob.

'This is what we are going to do,' he said, in a quieter tone, knowing that he didn't have to shout anymore to be heard. 'I will not have Alice hurt. As much as I detest your very existence in her life, it would destroy her to know what you are, so you cannot tell her, and no one else can know, so you need to manage that slut you are keeping.'

Jacob raised himself up to his true height. 'She's not a slut, John.'

The Viking king responded in kind and instantly towered over Jacob's false bravado. 'You have some fucking cheek, son, fucking fronting up to me. I will tear your cunting face off. Sit down, SIT FUCKING DOWN.'

Jacob did as he was told in an instant so that his lecture could continue.

'You have 12 months. That's time to build the business and sort out your double life. In 12 months we are going to talk about this, and if your affairs are not in order and Evan is not long gone, then I will take Alice from you, and bury you in a travellers' field.'

He reached down and grabbed Jacob's shoulder with such force that Jacob almost buckled in half like an accordion.

'Jacob, I can't emphasise this enough, do you understand me?'

Jacob nodded.

'Then I will say no more, and I will go and tend to my daughter before her big day begins. I'll see you out there, son. Don't let me down.'

What will you do now?

Jacob took a pocket square to the trickle of blood running down his forehead. *As we are told.*

We do not answer to him. I fear no physical power that he possesses.

Then what do you fear? Creature in my thoughts, voice that watches me trip up at every hurdle while apparently giving me advice to survive. What do you fear? WHAT?

WE FEAR EVAN!

You have no idea what you are doing, child

'Did I ever really know what I was doing?' Jacob voiced in reply.

Chapter 12: Sliding Doors

Song of the day: 'Touch Me I'm Going to Scream Pt. 2' by My Morning Jacket

Spring 2010

Faversham, Kent, UK

Look at you. Look at your skin as it catches the few rays of morning light trying to squeeze their way through the curtain break. You are beautiful, in a different way to Alice entirely, but no less so. I can't help but be mesmerised by the ringlets of blonde hair that fall so naturally, and how, even as you sleep in front of me, well, you look like you are posing for a shot. I'm waiting for you to open your eyes, so that I can kiss you without fear of waking you, because every girl who puts up with me must surely deserve more rest than others.

Jacob leaned over despite himself and gently laid his lips on her brow. He whispered *I love you* and slipped out of the bedroom. How had this happened to him? He had been through so much drama in his life – most of it caused by his own poor mindset, of course – that he didn't understand what he had done to deserve two beautiful women in his life, but he did have them, and he was happy.

He entered his kitchen in only his olive-coloured hipster briefs and danced a little as the stone tiles caught his bare feet off guard. He had always regretted not getting the underfloor heating here, as this kitchen floor was so beautiful he doubted it would ever be brought up for another. He methodically poured filtered water into his minimalist glass coffee jar and watched the drops of dark roast slowly fill the pot drip by drip. Jacob had always preferred the pour-over method of coffee-making. Yes, it took three minutes to get a cup, but the depths of flavour were the wake-up that his senses needed to take on the day. He hadn't heard Ahab in his mind for a few days, although he still jumped a little when the toaster broke the quiet perfection of the drip, drip, drip and spat out a slice of his home-baked loaf. He lavished its surface with salted butter and gripped it between his teeth while picking up both drinks.

The sensation of swapping from cold stone to warm carpet sent a tingle up his calves. He nudged the bedroom door open with his bottom as he entered the room backwards, and there he was, only his underwear to cover his shame as he stood, his large thighs constrained by the elastic and his flat stomach rippling with muscles that had only appeared since his dramatic boat diet two years before. With a milky tea in one hand and his drip-poured coffee in his right, he stood, toast in mouth, and marvelled at what lay before him. For as she lay, uncovered by sheet or clothing, a painted nail gently bitten in her mouth and her other hand squeezing the most perfect breasts Jacob had ever seen in life or for that matter on screen or in a magazine, she took Jacob's lust as she had taken his heart.

He placed the hot drinks and the toast on the bedside table, a piece of furniture he had taken from the boat he had been stranded upon. Then he leaned in and placed his lips on hers as he took his place above her, his hands exploring her body from her hips all the way up, until he pinned her arms above her head and entwined their fingers.

Her big eyes sparkled in the morning light as his tongue left her mouth with a gentle pull on her bottom lip.

'I can't believe the first time you say those words, it's when you think I'm asleep, Jay. Really, what is a girl to think?' Evan smiled innocently, which for her was never an easy feat, before leaning in for another kiss. Just before their lips touched, she whispered seductively, 'I love you too, Jay. I think I always have done.'

51

Look at you. Look at your skin as it catches the few rays of morning light trying to squeeze their way through the curtain break. You are beautiful, in a different way to anything I have ever deemed to fit that word. I can't help but be mesmerised by the colour of your hair, which is both the dark brown of your brooding father's and the autumnal fire of my own, and how even as you sleep in front of me, well, you look like you are a gift from heaven. I'm waiting for you to open your eyes, so that I can hold your little hand without fear of waking you, because every girl who puts up with me and your father surely deserves more rest than others.

Alice leaned over despite herself and gently covered Dorothy with the soft blanket she had kicked off during the night, before slipping out of the bedroom. How had this happened to her? She had been through so much drama in her life – most of it caused by her own poor mindset, of course – that she didn't seem to understand what she had done to deserve to have such a beautiful little woman in her life, but she did have her, and she was happy, she was sure she was, although still confused as to moving forward. Dorothy clung to her dad and could not speak a word to Alice, and, in turn, Alice had found it very hard to bond with her, although she knew it was early days.

Alice entered her parents' kitchen in her university hoodie and a pair of Jacob's old joggers. Her bare feet tingled and warmed as the stone tiles caught them off guard with the under-floor heating her father had fitted a few years back, apparently to help with his gout. He never complained about physical stuff much, so Alice couldn't argue with her father's expensive answer to his pain; it was his money, after all. She poured herself a green tea and threw some Cheerios into a bowl for Dorothy. She hadn't heard her stir just yet but knew it was coming. She may have struggled to bond with Dorothy – she still felt like she was looking after Jacob's child two days a week – but she had the heart of a mother, and taking care of Dorothy certainly wasn't a chore. Lost in her thoughts, she jumped a little when the toaster broke the silence and spat out a slice of Jacob's home-baked loaf. She lavished its surface with margarine and her mother's strawberry jam and gripped it between her teeth while taking her tea and Dorothy's breakfast back to bed.

The sensation of swapping from hard stone to the softness of the carpet in the hall sent a tingle up her calves. She nudged the bedroom door open with her bottom as she entered the room backwards, and... There he was, with only his underwear to cover his shame as he lay on his side upon Alice's bed, his chiselled body a patchwork of tattoos and his smile half hidden by his grey beard.

Alice dropped her tea, which smashed to the ground, quickly followed by the jam-covered toast.

William sprung to his feet. 'Are you OK? Let me help you.'

Alice looked around the room, noticing it to be the bedroom of the cottage in her dream.

'Dorothy!' she called as she ran out of the room, leaving William picking up the broken mug. Alice panicked. This was home, her make-believe home but her home, so there was no bedroom in which she would find her daughter. She darted from door to door, just to check her sanity wasn't as fractured as she feared, and found nothing. She ran back into the bedroom, where William was soaking up the green tea with a towel. She shrieked at what stood behind him, reflecting in the very mirror in which she had parted ways with Jacob's memory all those years ago. Her hair the red of grease and just as unclean, her flesh broken and unclean, her teeth rotten and broken apart from the pair of long pristine fangs either side of her forked tongue, which were highlighted all the more by the unnaturally large smile that this demonic version of Alice was always wearing.

'Alice, what's wrong?' asked William as she slumped to the floor in front of him, unable to breathe and unable to cry.

Welcome home, child, voiced the demon Alice with the wicked smile of the unclean.

Chapter 13: Johnno Was a Local Boy

Song of the day: 'Local Boy'
by The Rifles

End of summer 2007

Psychiatric Hospital of San Diego County,
California, USA

'What do you mean, she's pregnant?' asked Jacob.

'What I mean, Mr Brooking, is that we have had to put her into an induced coma due to her insistence on taking her own life, and this is more complicated due to the fact she is at least 16 weeks pregnant. You didn't notice your wife's small bump? Have there been any other signs, Mr Brooking?'

The woman tasked with minimising the damage Alice had done to herself just 12 hours before was Doctor Creed, the head of surgery. She was a woman of pure business – make-up free, hair impeccably scraped back. Everything seemed to be measured to perfection. Even the cactus on her desk sat upright at a perfect angle, and this was something that filled Jacob with the confidence he needed to get through the situation.

'No. I mean, I don't know. I've not been around so much the last three months. In fact, as I walked in on her cutting her throat, it was the first time I had seen her in 14 weeks.' Jacob fell into the seat opposite the doctor, completely bemused by the situation. 'Will the baby be OK?'

'The baby seems fine, and her heart rate doesn't appear to be affected at all by her mother's condition. If worst comes to worst and we can't get Alice right, then we can safely deliver like this, but let's hope we don't have to.'

Jacob wasn't listening. '*Her* heart? She's a girl?'

The doctor smiled. 'Yes, Mr Brooking. You are having a daughter.'

Jacob looked up, concerned. 'You seem to suggest she might not wake up. How much of a possibility is that? Please be honest.'

'I don't know any other way to be, Mr Brooking. But right now, nothing is certain. We don't expect anything to happen quickly. She needs to heal, both outside and in. Whatever demon she is trying to fight, we need to help her as best we can, and right now that means leaving her to rest.'

Over the Atlantic

'This is his fault, love, I'm telling you. It's that bastard Jacob, he's caused this.' John was livid. To hear that his Alice was in a critical condition had broken his heart, and John Petalow dealt with heartbreak the only way he knew how – with anger directed at the person he felt was responsible.

'You don't know that it's anything to do with Jacob. The last few times I spoke with Alice she seemed genuinely happy with everything, and I think Jay had a lot to do with that.'

Angela had always been John's voice of reason, but right now that wasn't going well with him.

'He is a drain on that poor girl's happiness, and you know it.' John spoke with the kind of tone that he usually reserved for the people who worked for him; it was rare for his wife to catch this end of the deal. 'Do you remember her as a teen? Always singing, always dancing. Everything she did had an aura of love and happiness. Where has that Alice been the last 15 years?'

'I know you don't like Jacob, I know you're worried about Alice. Do you not think I'm holding back the tears right now? Believe me, I am! But you are not helping, so shut up, remember you are a bloody Petalow, and get some rest.'

John knew better than to reply to this tirade from his wife. Instead, he tried to get comfortable so that he could sleep. The first-class seat was still too small for him; flying any other class wasn't even an option for him, as these were the only seats that fit him, bar the cargo hold. He downed the cheap bourbon that the flight attendant was claiming to be single malt whiskey and closed his eyes. *Bastard Jacob Brooking, ignoring my warning. I'll tear his arms off.* John drifted off with a wry smile, as he knew that was wholly possible for him to achieve. Unfortunately, he slipped into a dream that wasn't such a satisfying image.

He saw friends being killed in front of him. He saw the inside of HMS *Oberon*, the submarine that had been his prison for all those months. He and his very advanced Special Boat Service team had been on that sub in the Falklands during the summer of 1979, long before the war had started, and yet he still saw death.

Jacob Brooking stood there with him. The dead body of his daughter and the rest of C Squadron lay littered around them, mixed with the dead bodies of a dozen other submariners, butchered beyond all reason, with their throats cut or their hearts punctured. Jacob, wearing an Argentine uniform that seemed to fit him as if he'd been born into it, smiled with malicious intent. His hands were covered with blood, and at his feet was Alice, whose neck was broken and bloodied by a clearly one-sided struggle. John's heart started to race. He screamed his daughter's name and lunged at Jacob, but he was easily overpowered by a simple sweep of Jacob's arm, which brought him crashing to his knees.

'She's been mine for long enough now, Viking king. I will do with her as I please.'

In one motion, Jacob brought his hand down on John's exposed neck, meeting no resistance and taking his head clean off. John's decapitated head rolled like a hellish marble drawn from the nightmares of the damned until it came to rest next to the motionless body of his daughter, dead eyes looking back at his own, no speech able to escape his guillotined vocal cords.

As Jacob sat in the first-class waiting lounge, ready for the abuse he was sure to receive, he couldn't help but wonder what would have happened had he not returned to Alice. Was it his proximity to her that had made her do it? Could she sense him returning?

That's madness. I'm thinking like a madman. How could she have known I was coming? I saved her.

Jacob had been trying to convince himself of this for the whole journey to San Diego International, and he was no closer to succeeding after an hour of sitting at the bar, nursing a bourbon.

You're going to be a single father with a brain-dead wife. Good luck explaining that to the Viking, laughed the monstrous voice with a wicked cackle.

This wasn't my fault and you know it; Alice has always had her demons, just like I do.

Her demons didn't exist until she found out about Evan, or before you dragged her away from her family. Or shall we go further back, to when you bought a restaurant behind her back before convincing her to murder her unborn child? Was that not your fault either, Jacob? JACOB???

'WHAT?' shouted Jacob, much to the surprise of the barman, who had been minding his own business.

You know this is all on you

'But what the hell can I do about it now? I'm here, aren't I? Trying to make things right. What more can I do?' Jacob whispered to himself.

'You can start by bringing the car around to the front,' said a tired voice from behind.

Jacob turned to see Alice's mum standing there with her arms open.

'Hello Angela,' he said, jumping down from the bar stool to accept the hug he didn't realise he had needed. 'Where's John?'

'Getting the luggage sorted. He's... eager to see you. I guess that would be the way to put it.'

Angela found a false smile to go with this statement, but it did nothing to hide the reality of the situation. John Petalow wanted answers, and he would wring them from Jacob's neck if he had to.

Chapter 14: Nurse Bonnie

Song of the day:

'Don't Forget About Me'
by Cloves

Spring 2010

Canterbury, Kent, UK

Bonnie Belmonte had known the Petalows had money, but never had she expected such a beautiful home in such a rural location. Alice had been inviting her over for brunch every day since her release. They had grown quite close during her stay at the hospital, and there were only so many times Bonnie felt she could delay before Alice took umbrage at the excuses, so here she was. Bonnie knew it wasn't the most professional thing to visit a patient's home, but she had been eager to catch up with the gossip, and Alice had promised cake – and Bonnie Belmonte loved cake.

She pushed open the wrought-iron gate and marvelled at the beautiful garden, which was kept by a particularly green-fingered Angela Petalow. The pinks of lupins and the blues of delphiniums took her eye first, before the vivid red dahlias, which were arranged either side of the large oak door, actually gave her pause for thought and honest appreciation, especially as it was barely into March, a time when most other people's gardens were only just starting to bloom. Bonnie imagined that Angela's garden was like this all year round. *That's some voodoo gardening, I tell you, girl,* Bonnie thought as she knocked on the front door with a double crack of the brass door knocker.

There was no reply, other than the faint sound of Dorothy crying in the distance. Bonnie assumed that Alice was tending to her daughter and would be down in a moment. She rapped against the wood a second time, continuing to look around the wondrous garden. When her third knock went unanswered, curiosity got the better of her, and she started to stroll around the back of Manor Petalow.

'Alice, sweet child, are you to keep me waiting all day?'

At the rear of the house, large French doors overlooked an enormous back garden. Bonnie was about to call one last time, when Dorothy screamed from the window above her. She tried the handle of the back door and let out a sigh of relief when the door sprung open.

'Alice, are you OK, child?' called Bonnie, as she walked through the kitchen and made her way towards the large staircase and the source of the crying. All the doors on the upper floor were closed. She pushed open Dorothy's bedroom door. The child's face was flushed and full of the tears of a young girl too small to escape her bedroom yet old enough to know she had been left alone for longer than was normal.

'Hey, my littlest Brooking, what's wrong, my child?' said Bonnie as she reached down to pick Dorothy up from the ground.

Dorothy's little arms reached up to greet her saviour, her beautiful red hair unbrushed and matted with tears.

'Where's Mumma, my sweetness? Shall we go find her?'

Cradling her tightly, Bonnie took Dorothy out onto the landing. She noticed that one of the doors was in fact ajar, and that what was keeping it ajar was someone's foot. Without hesitation she rushed Dorothy back to her bedroom and sat her down on the bed.

'Dotty, my child, will you sit and play for just a few more minutes whilst I go get Mummy? I promise I'll be right back, and I'll leave the door open, OK?'

Dorothy nodded and crawled over her bed to hide under a mound of fluffy teddies, grabbing a regal-looking hare that sported a waistcoat en route.

Bonnie went back across the landing and entered the room where Alice was lying flat on her back. She knelt beside Alice and checked her pulse. She had seen her like this a thousand times, her eyes wide open and glossy but unresponsive and wider than looked naturally possible. Bonnie rolled her into the recovery position and placed a pillow from the bed under her neck.

'Alice, I know you can hear me, so do yourself a favour, poppet. Wake up before you fall too deeply. Do you really wanna lose another two years? No? I didn't think so. So, wake up.'

Bonnie was instantly back in work mode and her tone was strict and unwavering. She took out her phone, dialled 999 and asked for an ambulance.

'This is Sister Bonnie Belmonte of St Martin's Hospital. I'm with a patient of mine, Alice Petalow. We are just off Perry Lane at Preston Hill, the Petalow Manor, just by the large oak tree. It's set quite far back from the road, but you should find it at, erm, hang on...' She scrambled through her pockets to find the scrap of paper that she'd written Alice's address on. 'Right, at CT3 1ER. Alice is a mental health patient. She appears to have slipped into a catatonic state. She is breathing with a pulse of 65. I've tried to see if she is responsive to pain, but nothing so far. She doesn't appear to have self-harmed, so I've put her in recovery to continue my assessment.'

'Bonnie,' Alice croaked. She was struggling to pull herself up against the frame of the door. 'Bonnie, I – I slipped back into... I don't know how long I've been out. Where's Dorothy? Oh fuck, WHERE'S DOROTHY?'

Alice fell back down to her knees as Bonnie reached out to catch her.

'Take it easy, child, Bon Bon has got you.'

Bonnie led Alice to the bed and sat her upright, taking time to check her eyes and her breathing once more. 'Little Dotty is just fine, but I must confess, you have given me a scare. What was the last thing you remember?'

'I remember my alarm going off and I remember making

breakfast, then... then nothing.' Alice looked lost. 'I feel like I've been out for minutes, but you're here and my alarm went off at 7 a.m.'

'Then you have been out for about five hours, and that's OK because no harm was done. Paramedics are on their way – more than likely they will just want to check you over. Let me sort your little monkey out and I'll let them in when they arrive. Where are Dotty's bits?'

Alice looked guilt-ridden as she thought about the neglect of her daughter. 'Everything you need is in the storage cupboard outside her room. What do I tell Jacob when he arrives to get her later?'

Bonnie picked up Alice's chin with her index finger and whispered kindly, 'I'll worry about Mr Brooking, just like I have done for the past two years. Let's worry about you first, though, my sweetness.'

Chapter 15: Freudian Slip

Song of the day: 'Where I've Been' by Rival Sons

Spring 2010

Knightsbridge, London, UK

'Say it,' Dr Phillips demanded with force.

'I don't need to say it,' cried Alice. 'We both know what happened.'

'You need to say it, Alice. You give it power by protecting it.'

'I'm not protecting it. I'm not protecting him.'

'Say it, Alice.'

'I can't.'

'Say it!'

Alice was beside herself. 'I... I can't.'

One hour before

Alice loved her meetings with Dr Vivian Phillips, for she had known her so long that she was almost like family – she certainly felt closer to her than to any of her aunts and uncles. Alice wasn't stupid. She knew that she was paying – or, rather, her father was paying – for the privilege of being listened to. That being said, Alice felt she had a deeper connection than Dr Phillips' other patients would have with the esteemed psychologist. *After all*, Alice thought, *she knows my deepest, darkest secrets*. Her father had spent a fortune on her therapy and had never even met Dr Phillips, so Alice had to make this work.

'Why won't you talk about Thomas?' Dr Phillips asked astutely.

For a slight-framed, middle-aged woman, the good doctor was still the most frighteningly intimidating woman that you could hope to meet. Her £2,000 suit was not only immaculately fitted but pressed and ironed in a way that told Alice that it was done by a man who did it for a living. A lady of class like Vivian Phillips did not iron, press or even hang her own clothes; if Alice was sure of anything in this reality, it was that. But Alice wasn't intimidated by her, even if she knew just by looking at her that Vivian couldn't and wouldn't ever be messed with. The power radiated from her. But Alice knew there was a kind heart behind the professionally curled hair and Parisian styling, and she also knew that the reason Vivian always sat next to her, rather than across the breadth of the giant oak desk, was so that Alice felt like she was having a human conversation.

'Why don't we talk about the mirror once more? I feel like the depth of your issues are coming from there, and while your ability to change the subject is second to none, I think, deep down at your core, you know that this is where our focus should lie. So tell me, why do you think the mirrored reflection takes "your" form?'

Alice sighed. 'As I've mentioned before, it is, at least in my opinion, the reflection of the true character I am.'

'But Alice, you know that you have a kind heart, an intelligent and creative mind, and, let's be fair, most women would die for your figure and that gorgeous mane of auburn hair. So why would a diminished and almost demonic reflection be a personification of your true self?'

'People don't really look at me like that though, do they? I mean, after everything I've done.'

'What exactly do you think that you have done in this world to even make that statement, Alice? List off a few things.'

'Well, I mean Jacob wouldn't have strayed if I'd have been perfect, would he? And I was pretty easily convinced to give up my child.'

'We have been seeing each other long enough now that you know I'm not buying into any of this. Jacob's misgivings are not your fault. Jacob's decision to push for an abortion based on his own very poor choices was *not* your fault.'

'So, what do you think I see in the mirror? Because we have spoken before on this and normally you do more listening. Today I feel you are pushing me to say something.'

'Is there something you need to say? When you came out of that deep and dreadful sleep, you told me you were tired of protecting people. You know who you were talking about, don't you?'

'Thomas. I was talking… about Thomas.'

'Are you strong enough to hear my perspective on this? It will be something you don't want to hear.'

Alice nodded. Her hands became agitated, gripping her thighs through the denim of her jeans in the way a passenger might put their foot on an imaginary brake during a reckless driver's journey.

'I think you see yourself in the reflection because you find it easier to blame yourself than to blame Thomas for what he did. I believe the rotting flesh and broken teeth are a sign that you are trying to see through that image of yourself, that you want to blame his behaviour and free your conscience of the self-imposed guilt you currently feel. You know when you look at that monstrous reflection that it may look like you, but it's not you, it's Thomas, haunting you, mocking you. You have to free yourself of that blame.'

Alice looked up to see the doctor looking straight into her eyes as if her whole life was on display. 'But what if I was to blame? I mean... '

'Alice, you were not to blame. No woman deserves what you went through. Stop protecting him.'

'But I invited him round, when Jacob was working so hard and…'

'What happened, Alice? Say it,' Dr Phillips demanded with force.

'I don't need to say it,' cried Alice. 'We both know what happened.'

'You need to say it, Alice. You give it power by protecting it.'

'I'm not protecting it. I'm not protecting him.'

'Say it, Alice.'

'I can't.'

'Say it!'

Alice was beside herself. 'I... I can't.'

'SAY IT!'

'Thomas...'

'Thomas what?'

'Thomas...'

What did Thomas do, slut? I don't remember him doing anything

'What did Thomas do?' whispered Dr Phillips.

'Thomas Levit raped me,' Alice said, not realising that she had stopped crying.

Alice wandered about the large office, picking up various trinkets and ornaments from Dr Phillips' many trips around the globe. 'So, you want me to try and picture him, in the mirror, when I feel attacked.'

She was agitated, bordering on angry, and this was exactly what the doctor needed from her.

'In the long run,' said Dr Phillips, 'we need you to stop seeing anything in the mirror except your true reflection. Right now, I want you to start fighting the right battle, and it's not your own reflection you should be fighting, so push for him, when your demon self appears. Call him out, and I believe he will come.'

'Then that's what I will do,' said Alice gratefully. 'Thank you again.' She was standing on Dr Phillips' side of the desk. She picked up a picture in an ornate gold frame. It had a much younger Vivian Phillips atop a camel with another woman sitting behind her, embracing her waist like a koala scared to fall from a tree. 'Where was this taken?'

'Oh my, that would be 1975 I believe, in Cairo. A few years before you were born, Mrs Brooking.'

'It's Ms Petalow again, I'm afraid.' As she replaced the picture

65

and picked up the next, a photo in a much less elaborate frame, Alice caught her breath. 'But before we get on to Jacob, can you answer me this – why do you have a picture of this slut on your desk?'

Alice almost shattered the glass as she pointed at a very young, very innocent Evan Laurie.

Chapter 16: The Hand that Rocks

Song of the day: 'Sour Times'
by Portishead

Spring 2010

Faversham, Kent, UK

Jacob was called into work unexpectedly, and the moment he left, Dorothy started screaming. In the supermarket, she had a full-blown tantrum. Alice tried to control the situation by picking her up, but a distraught Dorothy kicked out aggressively, hurting Alice's chest. When they returned to Jacob's, Alice put her to bed in the hope that she would wear herself out, but young Dorothy showed unflagging commitment to the cause. The headboard cracked against the wall as Dorothy took her frustration out again and again on the frame of her bed. She lay on her back, kicking as if her life depended on it, while her tiny vocal cords provided the shrill noise of an ancient sea monster. How a child who had refused to speak to her since the day they had first met had the audacity to cry and scream at Alice was beyond her comprehension.

'This isn't real,' cried Alice. She gave up trying to calm her down and instead collapsed into the corner of Jacob's bedroom so as to completely shut herself down. She texted him to come home; he read but didn't reply to the message. She was on her own here, and she wasn't coping. All she could hear was the crash of the pine frame and the constant screaming, which was uncomfortably offset by one of Dorothy's toys playing 'Twinkle, Twinkle, Little Star' over and over on repeat.

'Alice, come home to us!'

The voice shouted passionately from everywhere and nowhere all at once. But it wasn't Alice's nightmare self.

'William, William, I can't cope, I don't know what to do.'

Alice cursed herself as she spoke, for she knew that William wasn't real, knew it was her own schizophrenia trying to find an angle into her fragile mind, but now, right now, she needed something; she needed him.

'Alice, I'm here, just follow my voice home.'

'William, I don't know what to do. She won't stop crying.'

'She's not real, none of this is. You have to find a way to see through this illusion of lies and mistruths.'

'I'm trying, baby, but I don't know how to do what you're asking of me. And I'm scared I'm going to do something that I will never be able to undo.'

'My beautiful and sweet Papillon. Remember what Doctor Phillips taught you. Think back to your safety training.'

Alice let out a whimper as she tried to gather the strength to follow through on William's plan. She took to her feet, clenched and balled her fists, drew a deep breath, and closed her eyes.

'That's it… Follow my voice, don't open your eyes… not until you feel me take your hand. Hold your grip tightly, and don't let go… Now tell me, Papillon… Can you hear the child crying now?'

'No, William, I don't think I can. Just that infernal nursery rhyme. It seems louder than ever.'

Alice, her eyes still shut and her hands still clenched, felt a calm wash over her.

'Then you are free, my sweet girl… Open your eyes…'

'ALICE! WHAT HAVE YOU DONE?'

Jacob's shout came out of nowhere as Alice realised that she had moved, unbeknown to her, straight to Dorothy's bedside.

Before she could see what she had done – she was gripping a pillow so tightly in her hands that blood, caused by her nails digging into her palms, was soaking through the material – Jacob thrust her aside, forcing her to crash heavily against the chest of drawers next to Dorothy's bed.

Dorothy wasn't moving. Jacob picked her up with one hand and ran from the room, dialling on his phone as he moved.

'Ambulance. Take my address first, 175 Hereford Close. It's my daughter, she's not breathing, I've just found her unresponsive.'

Alice slumped to the ground and started to shriek. She screamed and cried until her throat tore and the blood gargled in her mouth, and then she screamed again. She continued until the paramedic found her lying next to the foot of the bed. She didn't respond to the emergency doctor; why would she, when she hadn't even noticed Jacob rip the bloodied pillow from her hands moments before?

'Alice... I'm going to need you to calm down, or we might have to sedate you. Dorothy, your daughter, she's OK and she's breathing again.' The nurse took Alice by the shoulders and shook her upright. 'Alice, listen to me. She's going to be OK, so you need to calm down.'

'She's going to be OK,' Alice repeated.

'It looks to me like she smothered herself with one of the hundreds of soft toys in her bed. This isn't unheard of, Alice. It's not your fault.'

'She's going to be OK,' Alice repeated.

'Jacob has got into the ambulance with Dorothy and my partner to make sure that everything is tickety-boo. It seems like the little mite is enjoying all the fuss and attention.' The paramedic sat down beside Alice and nudged her gently with her shoulder. 'I'm not going anywhere, Alice, not until I know you're OK. As soon as you're ready, we can make our way to the ER.'

'Thank you,' croaked Alice.

The paramedic, a stern-faced brunette who had clearly hardened over years of service, flashed a small smile at her distraught patient. 'You and your partner did the right thing and called us right away. You saved your little girl by checking on her when you did.'

Guess you know now, spoke her nightmare self.

'It's all real,' cried Alice.

Now I wonder where you are, said Thomas in the dark of her mind.

Chapter 17: Evangeline

Song of the day: 'Wasting My Young Years' by London Grammar

Spring 2010

Knightsbridge, London, UK

'That "slut", Alice, is my daughter. Is this the Evan you have spoken about?'

Alice looked apologetic at the name-calling but stayed resilient in her tone. 'How would you not have picked up on that? It's hardly a common name.'

Vivian took a seat behind her desk and gestured for Alice to move to the sofa. 'I didn't realise because her name is not, and for that matter never has been, Evan. My daughter is Evangeline Phillips. If she has taken to being called Evan, it is clearly to try and upset me. We don't really talk anymore. I saw her once last year, in this very office, and that was it.'

'That would explain why she doesn't share your surname, either.' Alice was angry, but also frustrated that she had no place to direct the anger, with it clearly not being the fault of the doctor that her daughter was the woman she was.

'Tell me, what does she go by now? My daughter of a million masks.'

'Evan Laurie. And, yes, she is the one who stole my husband from me.'

'Evangeline Laurie Phillips – it's her middle name. The name I gave her to remember a love lost many years before. We... We are not as close as I would like. In fact, quite the opposite.'

'Is she close to her father?'

'Evangeline has never known her father, and maybe my dedication to forging this career is what pushed her away. You might hate her, Alice, but my daughter has been moved from nanny to nanny, from boarding school to university. She is truly loved, but she doesn't know love, not like you do. I won't ever excuse her actions. For many years we fought like cat and mouse as I tried to curb her affections for always getting her own way. But I will say this. When I saw her last year – when she sat in the very chair you are sitting in now – she spoke as a woman who was genuinely in love. It was a side of her I've never seen, and it made me happy.'

Doctor Phillips stood proudly and came around to offer her hand to Alice. 'Unfortunately, I feel this situation now compromises our relationship and concludes our business here. If you need further help, then I have a list of people you can speak to, but honestly... I think you've got this.'

Part Four
The *Kraken* Released

Chapter 18: Take Me Back

Song of the day: 'If I Go, I'm Going' by Gregory Alan Isakov

Winter 2009

Knightsbridge, London, UK

'What's the last thing you can remember clearly from San Diego that you know with absolute certainty was a memory of reality and not the false perception that you then started to build for yourself?' asked Dr Phillips without once taking her eyes off Alice, who was stretched out, eyes closed, on the long leather sofa.

'You are asking what you think is a simple question, but in all honesty it may be the hardest thing I've ever had to answer, for what is real in my head has often been what has led me astray. You have to understand that if I didn't see Jacob standing in front of me, breathing in front of me, then I can tell you now as a matter of fact that I saw him die and it was real.' Alice took a deep breath before she continued. 'My memories do not come at me like I was in a dream, for I do not see blurred lines, faint sounds and vacant tastes. I must confess that as crazy as it seems, I see only reality in what I saw, like looking at a photo album – I see every colour clearly, see every face and hear every seagull that would mercilessly fight for the leftover croissant that I swear I can still taste the remnants of.'

'The problem you have is your own imagination. I have sat here with stupid people, people with far too much money who think they have the same problem you have, but they don't have the mind to

75

create the world that your fabulous mind has created. Your world-building is second to none, and that's why you struggle. So instead of looking at what looked like or had the smell of a reality that your mind could easily build, I want you to look at something else.'

'Which is?'

'It's fairly textbook that the things that happened in your false reality were created to solve the issues in your heart. Your mum died because you felt you had let her down. She had been married for decades, put up with all your father's tantrums and mood swings. Didn't you mention he had PTSD from his time in the navy?'

'I did, yes.'

'You felt like you had let her down by not surviving the marriage like she had. Jacob's death was no different. Yes, you were mad at him for what he did to you, but ultimately you just wanted him to be at peace, and you didn't know how to solve his issues without laying him to rest. The art studio had always been a dream of yours. You told me that in session one. So, is it any surprise that you ended up there?'

'And William?'

'The looks of a Greek god, tattoos and a six-pack. He's educated, a millionaire, and he works with endangered animals for a living.'

Alice sat up and opened her eyes. 'It's too perfect.'

'Of course it is. William wouldn't exist in any reality except a false one, or I wouldn't be gay, Alice.'

Alice paused for a moment, slightly taken aback by this revelation. 'So, what do I need to look for?'

'You are looking for what didn't look real. You need to reverse that. Start looking for things that were not part of your script, little moments that surprised you because they were never part of your plan. What do you remember of Jacob that you saw in San Diego, that you never could have seen coming?'

Winter 2006

San Diego, California, USA

Alice had been holding tightly onto Jacob's arm for the duration of the long walk home from the French restaurant in town. The air was warm even in December, but struggling to get out of the British mentality of what winter was all about, she had worn a pink glittery bobble hat and equally vibrant scarf to accessorise her white cashmere sweater and matching jeans. Jacob had taken them out to celebrate her first commission coming in. The fact that she was painting again had given Alice an almost childlike happiness. She would bounce around the house, constantly sketching and screaming out ideas. This was the Alice he had fallen in love with all those years ago, the Alice that he had treated right and the Alice he wanted to spend his life with. They danced through the night to imaginary tunes they were playing through their minds, and the clicks of their heels fell in time with every step. They loved each other. Although those feelings were also false due to the nature of what was to be revealed some months later, the situation was real, and what Jacob was to say next would change Alice's opinion of her husband forever.

'Baby, baby, stop.' He ground to a halt, pulling Alice round to face him.

She smiled. 'Hey you.'

'Baby…' Jacob hesitated, his words choking him up from inside.

'Jay, what is it? Talk to me.'

'Alice, I'm really sorry… I've been thinking about everything, everything that brought us here, to this place.'

'San Diego? It was a plane, my love,' said Alice playfully, before noticing tears rolling down his cheeks. 'Jay, you're scaring me. What's wrong?'

'I'm sorry that I made you give up our child. I've regretted it every day since, and I see you walking into that hospital every time I close my eyes.' Jacob trembled, as if voicing his true self made him vulnerable. 'It haunts me in my day and more so in my dreams.'

'You didn't MAKE me do anything. Where has all this come from?'

'We are both aware that had my outlook been different, then we would be pushing a pram right now. It was my broken mind that talked us out of that choice, and I can't take it back, I can't...'

Jacob was quickly becoming inconsolable. He fell to the floor and wrapped himself around Alice, who crouched down to join him.

'Oh sweetheart,' she said, 'we can't know what would have happened. Whatever has led us here has worked out for a reason. We could have had that child and broken up a month later. Who knows if I can even carry successfully after...' Alice realised her thoughts had drifted away from her. 'You just don't know. But, baby, I do know this...'

Jacob responded by gripping Alice a little tighter.

'I know that I love you,' she went on, 'I know that I'm happy, and I know that "where we are" is a beautiful place.'

'You mean San Diego?' asked Jacob with a whimper.

'No, you bellend, I mean us, where WE are, is beautiful!'

Jacob lay there, safe within Alice's warm embrace, while the ocean lapped the shore to their right. Neither of them said a word. Alice occasionally kissed Jacob's brow, and they didn't let go. It felt like home.

Knightsbridge, London, UK

'I hated seeing him upset, but at the same time I don't think I've ever loved him more, or even known him more. That Jacob there was the Jacob I never expected to see.'

'You had seen him cry before, though, held him as his heart broke?'

'But this was the first time I'd ever heard him tell me honestly why he was hurting. That I think is the most real memory I have from San Diego. I got to see the man I love for the first time, and I got an apology I both didn't expect and didn't know I needed.'

'What are you feeling now, Alice?'

'Like I want to remember more!' said Alice with a renewed fire in her eyes.

Chapter 19: Love and the Locker Room

Song of the day: 'I Got the…'
by Labi Siffre

Spring 1996

Canterbury, Kent, UK

Alice had been battered during what had been the most intense 60 minutes of lacrosse she had ever played – a 13-9 loss to a Maidstone side that, on a different day, couldn't have held a candle to the league leaders at Canterbury WLC. Alice was only playing in the colts, as she was still short of 18, but the side she had faced today had been full of adults each a little quicker and more educated on tactics. The freeze pack on her knee was starting to become useless as the afternoon sun, on a particularly warm May afternoon, melted the ice quicker than she could replace it. Another graze on her forearm would need cleaning when she got back to the locker room; Alice had picked most of the gravel out, but she could feel throbbing as though a foreign object was lodged deep inside her skin. Alice was normally the motivational coach for the locker room. She was the club's top scorer, at least in the colts, and found it easy to give the pre-match pep talk, but today she was struggling to find a good reason why she wasted her Saturday afternoons getting beaten up with hard balls and harder sticks.

'You looked good today, Pebble. Just wasn't your day, I guess,' said Jacob as he joined Alice on the sidelines and took her hand into his own.

'Our bloody defence let us down again, but can you blame them when the opposition is fielding a team of semi-professional players? Thank you for coming to watch me though, bubba. It means a lot, even if we lost. I know you don't get much time off.'

'Don't be silly. I only took that job to shut your father up, so getting to watch his daughter run around in these little shorts for an hour is kind of bliss, to be honest.' Jacob tugged at the waistband of a figure-hugging pair of white shorts.

'Baby, please come back home and find something in Canterbury,' pleaded Alice as she discarded the ice pack. 'I know you are doing well, but I can't see why you have to be stuck out there on the outskirts of London.'

'I promised your father a year, and I want to prove the old fool wrong. And things are going bloody well. Who would have guessed? Jacob Brooking, young chef of the year.'

'I am proud of you, Jay; I just miss you. It's unfair that I must be alone whilst all those waitresses get to flirt with you every day.'

'Even if that were true, do you honestly think that I could ever have eyes for anyone but you? Never could I find such beauty in another, my love.'

Jacob went down on one knee in a mock proposal, and Alice reacted by pushing him over for trying to be funny.

'You'd better get cleaned up if you want us to spend some time together before the Viking king takes you away from me,' said Jacob from his new position on the Astroturf.

'Yes, boss,' replied Alice, bending over to kiss Jacob firmly on the lips. 'I'll be quick.'

'Great game, losers! Reminded me of when we were kids playing junior league,' taunted a spiteful blonde who could only be a year or two older than Alice. 'Hey, ginge, good job missing that open goal at the end. Real classy bit of play to spoon it into the crowd.'

'If you call the group of boys getting far too excited about your bust a crowd, then, yeah, I guess you are right, blondie,' retorted Alice with a smile.

'The fuck you say to me? You snotty bitch, I will wipe the smile off your face before I go out there and fuck that cute little thing that was watching you.'

The blonde girl rounded on Alice but got no rise from her, as Alice refused to take her head out of her locker.

Coward, the voice whispered.

'I didn't say anything,' said Alice. 'Anything at all actually. You must have misheard me.'

'That's right, you misheard her, blondie. So why don't you climb back onto your coach and fuck right off,' said Holly, Alice's best friend and the club's vice captain.

'Or what?' snapped the blonde. 'You gonna eat me, tubs?'

Holly stepped forward, towering over her much slighter opponent. 'Oh, you fucking wait and see what I do.'

'Come on, Laurie, let's leave the kids to play with each other, yeah,' said one of the older girls. She pulled the blonde round and shuffled her out the door.

'Take care, ladies,' said the Maidstone captain, who was the last of the opposition to leave the locker room.

'See you later, bitches.' Holly waved as she bounced her curvaceous hip off of Alice, almost knocking her into her locker.

'Yeah, see you in the play-offs, ladies,' said Alice. She pulled off her kit and dumped it in a pile on the floor. 'Why does everyone we ever speak to have to treat us like we're a bunch of weak-willed fairies?'

Holly laughed. 'You speak for yourself, ginge. I don't get much trouble.'

'That's because you look like a hungry, hungry hippo when you're pissed off, Holl.'

'You little...'

Holly was cut off by sounds of laughter from outside and went to see what the commotion was, while Alice struggled to get a towel around her.

Jacob was sitting next to, and talking to, the blonde. She laughed and touched his arm before bouncing up and heading over to the coach.

Alice tripped over herself as she tried to get her jogging bottoms on. 'What's going on out there, Holl?'

'Nothing. Just Jacob talking to himself and the Maidstone bitches all trying to squeeze those big heads onto the coach.'

'He does that a lot,' said Alice, wondering how much of her boyfriend's craziness she should divulge in public.

'Babe, you knew Jay was crazy when he met you. Don't pretend this is a new thing.'

Alice's inner voice started to laugh with a dry rasping cackle. She looked at herself in the locker-room mirror as she threw some perfume on and tied her hair back. *That will have to do*, she thought.

The mirror's reflection of her was moving a fraction slower than she was – a vision that didn't change as she rubbed her eyes and tried to regain her focus.

He's not the crazy one... is he?

Chapter 20: Brand-New Start

Song of the day: 'It's Gonna Be (Alright)' by Ween

Spring 2010

Canterbury, Kent, UK

I'm going away. I know what you're thinking. You think I'm abandoning my responsibilities, you think I'm running away from my problems, but you are wrong, you are all wrong. I have been asleep for two long years, and by all accounts I've been mentally ill for a lot longer than that. But while your worlds kept on moving, mine did not. My real world froze, while I started my own business, met the man of my dreams and lost my two best friends in a fantasy my over-creative mind had drawn up from my deepest fears and highest aspirations. And now… I'm a mum to a beautiful daughter whom I don't remember carrying. I have no business, and yet I remember building it from scratch…

Let's not forget Jacob

And my husband, my soulmate, the man I saw die in my arms, is now in a happy relationship with the woman he cheated on me with, and I cannot process that. I can't fathom why you would do that to me, Jay, I just can't. And yet you seem happier than I've ever seen you before. You, Jacob, Mr Never-happy-with-anything-he-has. Always chasing more, always wanting more. And now…

Now he's happier without you

Now you are content for the first time in your life, and with the only woman I've ever hated. Jacob, I need to do this, and you know I'm right. I've found a little retreat on the beach, a place I can paint and read whilst my memories come back, where I can find myself once more. I need this, and I think you know that Dorothy needs that from me too.

Dorothy will grow to resent you, as will your mother

Mum, don't be upset. We can write every week. And I want to keep you and Dad apprised on my progress. I want to be able to communicate more about some of the things I've been through, and that will only happen if we are all willing to work together.

They will forget you. Remember when you were in a co*ma? They pretty much adopted Jacob and Evan*

Dad, after all these years I still can't tell if your silence means you are angry or proud of me, so I'm just going to presume that at least you understand.

All he understands is that his happy family was more co*mplete while you were asleep*

And my beautiful little girl... I can't convey my feelings for you because I don't understand them, but as I look at your auburn ringlets falling around your neck and I look into your eyes, a deeper blue than mine have ever been and circled by a band of emerald that reminds me of your father every time I look at you, I do know that I want to do everything I can to make you happy, make you safe and make you loved.

Her stepmum will love her more than you ever could

Alice took a deep breath, the last comment taking its toll on her heart with the bitter truth than ran through it. She took the door handle in her hand and tried one last time to regain her composure. 'You've got this,' she whispered to herself before she entered the room full of false confidence. Her parents were there, laughing with Jacob as Dorothy waddled between them all, trying to catch a balloon that bounced above her head, her laughter infectious and impossible to ignore.

'Hey, you guys, thank you for coming,' said Alice, drawing everyone but Dorothy's attention. 'We need to talk. No, that's not right, not at all. What I mean is... I need to tell you something.'

Autumn 2010

Old Salty Cottage
Melville Drive
Sandown
I.O.W.
PO22 8SW

Dearest Dotty

Your father has promised me that he's reading you these, so with that in mind I want him to give you a big fat kiss when you get to the bottom. I want you to know that I miss you terribly and that I'm safe and enjoying the sand between my toes. It is my hope that one day I can bring you back here, so that you can see where I found my way once more. I hope Nanna and Poppa Bear are OK, and that you are looking after your dad. He struggles to even make his bed without a strong woman by his side, so keep on top of him for me, will you?

I look outside and I see the leaves are falling and changing into the colours that match both your hair and your fiery temperament, and it reminds me what a beautiful and amazing thing that I have created in you.

I have sent you some shells I collected from the beach. Ask your dad to put them on your bedroom window for me, so that when you look outside you know that I am thinking of you.

I miss you.

Mum
(Ask Dad to kiss you)

Chapter 21: Release the Kraken

Song of the day: 'Sweet Pea'
by Amos Lee

Summer 2010

The coastal roads of east Kent, UK

Jacob knew it was there and yet couldn't quite focus on the bastard creature that had followed him all these years. The shadow it cast was unnatural in so many ways, like spilt ink over a photograph of the room, and it had always been the same. As Jacob approached his 30th birthday, he had noticed the creature's physical presence less each day, maybe due to his ever-increasing tolerance of its presence. He still hated the creature and was always wary of its place in the day, for it never appeared without reason or purpose, and neither of those things were ever really a positive.

'It's not like you to hide, Ahab. What's so wrong that you have taken to skulking around the shadows looking for carrion to pick at? I thought you were a predator. No? My mistake.'

Jacob mocked the creature slightly but still had an air of caution in his voice. He had played this game for long enough now to know it could change in an instant. Content that the kraken, Ahab, would stay hidden under his bed, he carried on getting dressed, finishing his tie with a half-Windsor knot.

'I'll catch you later, old man,' Jacob whispered, patting the bed on his way out of the bedroom. 'Was a pleasure talking to you.'

He heard only a barely audible grumble in reply.

'Are you ready, ladies?' called Jacob excitedly as he bounced down the stairs.

At the bottom, he was confronted by a vision that just a few years ago he could never have imagined he would see, and it warmed his soul that he knew with complete certainty that this was a reality he had built and not destroyed.

'How do we look, Dad?' said Evan.

She twirled round in a circle, holding in her arms a giggling Dorothy. They were dressed in identical summer dresses of yellow and gold, with their hair tied up and bound by gold ribbon.

'You look... Well, you look perfect to me. I truly am a lucky man to have you both with me.'

Jacob had organised a day of taking photos at a little spot called Samphire Hoe on the Dover and Folkestone borders. A man-made beach that had been developed using the soil dug out when the Channel Tunnel was built back in the mid-1980s, since 1997 it had been a fantastic tourist spot, especially for those with a keen eye and a good lens.

On the drive down, Dorothy and Evan sang nursery rhymes until the journey got too much for the littlest Brooking, and she fell asleep with her fingers in her mouth and dribble on her chin. Evan then pulled herself a little closer to Jacob, while he navigated the coastal roads with more care than he would have done in his old Benz. He had decided to get something family sized when he had become a father, and the big BMW X5 didn't cling to the road as much as his old coupé when driven at speed, although Evan had commented that since becoming a father, he had slowed down naturally anyway, and she had assured him that was for the better, as it was his whole lifestyle that had slowed down.

'I fucking love you, Jay,' said Evan under her breath, knowing Dorothy could be listening. 'This has felt so different, these last few years... This "us". You know?'

Jacob gave her thigh a little squeeze. 'I know exactly what you mean, love. Who would have thought openness and honesty would have made me a more lovable man, right?'

Although Jacob was smiling, he knew there was a modicum of

truth behind his statement, and clearly Evan knew it too, as she squeezed his hand in return.

'You didn't know you were poorly, babe,' she said, 'although why you kept it from me I'll never understand. But let's be fair, I was no saint either, and I didn't make it easy on you.'

Jacob was waiting for the creature to cut in at any point, but every pause in the conversation brought only silence. 'Easy on me? Honey, I was petrified of you!'

Evan looked at Jacob in disbelief. 'Petrified? But you are so much bigger than me. What could you have feared?'

'Back then I couldn't deal with confrontation as most people do, you know this, but maybe subconsciously I was also scared I was losing you.' Jacob seemed like he was struggling to admit his past feelings, but spoke without prompt. 'Ev, I convinced myself that what we had was nothing so that it was justified in my head, that the affair was acceptable. But I see now that, actually, I was much more myself by your side than I'd ever been with anyone else.'

Evan smiled and pushed her head into Jacob's shoulder. 'Well, if it led us here, to where we are now, then I wouldn't change a thing.'

'Nearly dying on that bloody boat wasn't much fun, but, yeah, I agree.'

The car went into the steep drop of the tunnel that led down to the beachfront, causing everyone's stomachs to flip for a moment. Dorothy's eyes shot open in a wide stare, shocked at the sudden lurching feeling.

'It's OK, poppet,' said Evan, turning to face her at the sound of a whimper, but she had already drifted back off into whatever fairy-tale dream could occupy the mind of a two-and-a-half-year-old girl.

With Dorothy asleep in the car, Evan and Jacob started to unload the picnic basket and camera from the boot of the car, sharing a kiss in between every little task they performed. As Jacob pulled the boot closed, he leaned into Evan and kissed her with such force that she fell against the car, his hands pinning her in place.

'Wow, where did that come from?' said a startled Evan in

between more kisses peppered upon her lips by an almost rampant Jacob.

'I just wanted to show you what I thought of you before I showed you this.'

Jacob pulled away, one hand still on Evan's hip. He reached into his back pocket and pulled out a sealed letter with Alice's name on it.

'Baby, I don't understand,' said Evan, recoiling slightly at the sight of Alice's name. 'What's that got to do with me?'

'This is a signed copy of my divorce papers, and if you help me with a task over the coming months, I'd like to post them through Alice's door, because when I propose to you, I'd like to do it as a free man.'

'PROPOSE?' said Evan. 'When you propose?'

Her mouth was agape. She jumped up into his arms, wrapping her legs around him as he spun about, kissing her pink glossy lips.

'Jay, you have completed me. I'll do anything to spend my life with you both.'

As Evan's feet slowly came back down to earth, and Jacob's kisses became deeper and more passionate, he waited for the voice of Ahab to offer its opinion. He waited, and yet… It never came.

Chapter 22: Step by Step

Song of the day: 'Grow As We Go' by Ben Platt

Spring 2011

Sandown, Isle of Wight, UK

'Good morning, Mrs Frodsham,' called Alice as she skipped along the road past the old cottage. 'How are the flowers today?'

Mrs Edna Frodsham had been Alice's neighbour since she had moved here and had never been anything less than hospitable. It was no rare occurrence to see her appear at the back window with a freshly made gypsy tart or Bakewell slice. 'Another week or two before we hit any kind of real bloom, my dear. You make sure you keep warm, pet. It's blowing hard down on the front.'

'I will, Mrs Frodsham, I promise.'

Alice carried on down the road. Her purple bobble hat wasn't really needed, especially as she didn't feel cold today, but it matched her scarf, and she hadn't been able to do much with her hair to stop the wind whipping it up like candyfloss on blustery days like this. She took the cobbled steps down to the seafront, where she had made her home the past five months. Both her fitness and her equilibrium had returned fully after "the long sleep", as she had described it to her local doctor, and with little effort she bounced from stone to stone without catching the crooked and broken edges that had caught her out so many times when she had first arrived. Her Converse trainers sunk into the sand as soon as she reached the bottom, and she instantly regretted not wearing her boots on a day that, although not cold, was far too brisk to go barefoot.

She turned to her right and followed the chalky rock face for 30 minutes before finding the spot she needed, a place where no one else could see her. Her own spot – not one borrowed from Jacob or imagined in her fantasy, just hers. She had come here every day the weather had allowed since her arrival, but today was different, today was special, and she intended to mark the occasion. She took the last few steps towards the final part of her journey. Two large slabs of rock that had fallen from the cliff face many hundreds of years before were her destination. One was curved in the middle and had the look of a fancy chair designed for the aristocracy; the other was more jagged and held anything that Alice wanted to sketch while sitting in her royal chair.

She sat down and took out her sketchbook. She flicked through the pages, seeing numerous drawings she had made of shells and driftwood over the months. Even a crab claw, mottled and dyed by the sun's rays, had found a place in Alice's work. She found the last page completely empty and pulled out a black ballpoint to rectify that.

Dearest Alice

In finishing this book, you have completed the first step of your recovery.

You remember once again all that is real and all that is not.

You remember you. Now finish this.

Alice M Petalow
29/4/11

As soon as the date was written, Alice closed the book and took the deepest breath she had ever taken. *This is it, girl. Remember what everyone kept saying. You've got this.* Reaching into her satchel, she took out an aggressive-looking camping knife and removed the safety cover. *You've got this.* She furrowed out a space under the second slab of rock with the blunt edge of the blade, deep enough to fit her leather-bound sketchbook. She forced the sketchbook underneath the large monolith before covering the entrance with loose sand until no trace of it could be seen. *You can do this, Alice,* she reassured herself over and over. She sat back in her cold, hard seat of queens and leaned forward with the knife in her hand. *Last step... You've got this...* With a final push, she took the sharp edge of the curved blade and very slowly started to carve her initials into the rock that protected her work. 'Time to go home, Alice,' she said confidently to herself.

A M P

29/4/11

Canterbury, one week later

Alice stood with her key in the door. She hesitated, for she knew what was waiting on the other side of it. *You've got this,* she thought to herself as the lock turned with a triple click.

'I'm home, guys. There had better be either a kettle on or a glass of wine poured ready for me.'

There was no response.

'Hellooooooo... Anyone home?'

She was met with the same lack of response as before.

'Welcome home, Alice,' she said to herself sarcastically, while picking up the post from the floor. Three letters for Dad; one for Dotty, which was clearly a delayed letter that Alice had sent a week before; and one for Mrs Alice Brooking. It had been some time since Alice had referred to herself by her married name, so it made her anxious to consider the contents.

It looks official. It could be anything, Alice mused. It could be a doctor's appointment. Yes, that must be what it is.

Alice took a seat on the third step of the stairs – a step that in her youth she had considered her thinking step – and tore open the letter. She read the lines, 'In the family· court at Canterbury City, between Alice Marie Brooking and Jacob Paul Brooking...'

Chapter 23: The Little Butterfly

Song of the day: 'Don't Know Why' by Norah Jones

Spring 2012

Faversham, Kent, UK

A year had passed since she had posted back the signed divorce papers, since she'd had anything substantial to do with Jacob, save for Dorothy's birthday party and her infant-school induction. Alice really had no reason to do anything except exchange pleasantries at the midweek handover. She had been polite, more than polite; after all, she got a four-figure cheque through the post each month for her share of the Gallantry. But a kiss on her cheek would be standard, before he would take her hand and tell her she was doing 'really well' – patronising bastard. She wasn't doing well at all, and what right did he have to tell her what he perceived? He certainly had no right to touch her with those dirty and sullied hands, surely thick with the stench of that harlot.

Today it changed. Today she would be honest with him, hear his voice tremble as she released years of built-up angst against his and Evan's false relationship. It had been building.

Her monster still spoke to her every day. Knowing her monster was a representation of Thomas had given it a name, but it hadn't stopped the noise. And she was tired of carrying around her demons. She was tired full stop. Today was the first day of clearing out her closet.

Knock, knock, knock.

He's probably fucking Evan

KNOCK, KNOCK, KNOCK.

That's *it, knock louder, because that will stop him*

KNOCK, KNOCK…

'Alice, what the actual fuck? Use the bloody doorbell, that's what it's for. What on earth is wrong?'

Alice glanced to her right and saw the brass button, but it only took a second to remember why she was banging in the first place, and she quickly turned her attention back to Jacob.

'You're engaged?' said Alice with disgust.

'Erm… I guess I am. I was going to tell you when I dropped Dotty off tomorrow.'

'Well, you don't have to worry now, do you? I ran into Matt yesterday, and he seemed oblivious as to who he was talking to as he detailed how he had never seen "chef" happier than he had recently.'

'Alice, I'm not sure what you're so unhappy about? We've been separated years.'

And whose choice was that?

'And whose choice was that, Jay? Because it wasn't mine.'

'Alice, stop! I'm not that guy anymore, and do you know what? You are not this girl anymore. So stop and come with me.'

Jacob grabbed his car keys and a second set that she didn't recognise and closed the door behind him.

'I'm not going anywhere with you,' she said.

Jacob opened the passenger door and offered his hand to Alice. 'Just get in the bloody car, love.'

Alice ignored his help and climbed into the car with a slam of the door and a grunt of derision. Jacob looked at the sky and pleaded for a little mercy on his day off, but he knew it wouldn't come.

'Where are we going?' asked Alice. 'Because I can't see what on earth you might think I would care about now.'

Jacob summoned a false smile and took a breath. 'You sound

more like your father every day. Just have a bit of faith, will you?'

Alice looked out of the window as the car pulled away, hoping that a tornado would appear, as though they were in an L. Frank Baum novel, and suck them off this plane of existence. This world was just a little too painful for Alice right now, and she felt exposed by its reality.

'I don't get it,' she said. 'I don't get Evan and all her little quirks that seem to make everyone hate her but you. I've never seen you so happy and so bloody composed. You have even left your demons behind, and that's something I just can't explain.'

'Me either, and neither should I have to. I know it makes no sense to you, but honestly I just feel more myself with her, and I can be more myself around her. And you know what? I am happy. Is that so wrong? I mean, I want no different for you, after all.'

Alice scowled but didn't take her eyes off the sky. 'How very magnanimous of you.'

'All that matters now is we try to do what's right by Dorothy, and that's what this is all about.'

Jacob pulled into the tiny parking space behind the row of vintage shops on Whitstable high street and jumped out onto the cobbled streets. 'Well, are you coming?'

'Do I have a choice?' answered Alice.

Good job putting him back in his place, bitch

'Jacob, what have you done?'

Alice looked up as he pulled away the plastic protection of the brand-new shop sign: 'Le Petit Papillon'.

It wasn't identical to the font in her false reality, but it was close.

'We have built your shop into the old sewing-machine building. It's near identical to the one you built in your dreams.'

'But how did you know?'

'We've been making notes. Me, your mum and dad – actually, everyone you have spoken to about your dream world. I guess we've just figured it out between us.'

'My parents knew about this?'

'Yes. It was my idea. But it was your father who told me I had

97

to do something for you in return…'

'In return for what?'

'For your share of the restaurant. We valued it at £180,000. This shop has cost slightly more, but this has given you licence to be free once more.'

'The little butterfly,' whispered Alice.

'That's Dorothy, right?'

'Yes… Of course that's Dorothy. How many other little butterflies do you know? Shall we take a look inside?'

Alice was almost speechless when she saw the interior of the shop. 'Jacob, I don't know what to say.'

'Well, thank your dad more than me. He did more of the painting and woodwork. We were going to do a grand unveiling tomorrow, but since you came knocking at my door… I didn't really have much of a choice.'

'I am still mad at you,' Alice said without looking him in the eye. 'You can't keep buying your way out of everything.'

'I am not buying anything. This has been bought by your shares in the company,' Jacob said with authority.

'And what if I choose not to take this on? After all, you can't make me give up my shares!'

'No, Alice. No one can make you do anything. Have we ever been able to make you do anything against your will? Christ almighty, Pebble, we couldn't even make you wake up before you were ready!'

'Don't call me that, Jacob. My name is Alice. Now answer the question – what will you do if I don't take it on?'

He sighed. 'Then me and your father will have to share a tear-filled hug and I will have to put the bloody building back on the market.'

Alice's eyes glazed over. She picked up a photo from the counter. The photo was of a black-and-red butterfly on a piece of driftwood – a photo she had taken many years before down at Rye Harbour.

'I love it,' she said. 'I hate you for taking the fire out of my voice today. I hate you for asking that tart to marry you. I hate you for being happier with her than you were with me. But I love this.'

'So we have a deal? If so, the building is yours. I've paid the rates and council tax for a year. All it needs is your touch of magic and those bloody amazing pictures hung on the walls.'

'Thank you, Jay. I do really appreciate what you and my parents have done here.'

'It's my pleasure. Just make sure you invite me to the opening.'

'Of course.' Alice laughed. 'Just don't bring that –'

Jacob cut her off quickly. 'Before you say anything more, I want to say one thing. Her life, although strange and vulgar to you, has not been easy. I love her, and she is wonderful with Dorothy.' He handed the keys of the property over to Alice. 'You might find that you have more in common than you think.'

Chapter 24: The Bride

Song of the day: 'Save Me from Myself' by Christina Aguilera

Autumn 2012

Tunbridge Wells, Kent, UK

Evan looked in the mirror and saw every negative that had been pointed out by men over the years. Her bust was escaping her dress and her hair was struggling to stay up in the fashion in which she had intended, her blonde locks being of such length that even when they were curled, their weight was constantly trying to bring them down. Her bright red lips were matched by her six-inch heels, while the rest of her look was that of traditional ivory.

'You can do this, Evangeline. He loves you exactly how you are, remember? He knows your past, and you know his.'

'Evan, you look amazing, you old tart,' said Heather as she fell into the room, with a half-empty bottle of prosecco gripped tightly in her hand.

'Hev, if you are pissed on my bloody wedding day, I will never forgive you!'

'I'm not pissed. I just can't walk in these bloody heels you bought me.'

If one was to describe Evan as a flamingo, then Heather was certainly an ostrich. She was larger than Evan in both physical appearance and personality.

'Heather, you look beautiful,' said Evan. 'Now pour me a glass of that, will you? I am shitting myself here.'

Heather poured a tall glass of prosecco and dropped in a fat strawberry from the breakfast basket for good measure. 'There we go, chuck, but I don't; you do. You look amazing. And you know what?'

'What's that, babe?' said Evan while downing the glass of prosecco.

'He fucking loves you, girl. I didn't think so before, but watching him interacting with you these last few years – well, he never takes his eyes off you. Or his hands, for that matter!'

'I know he loves me. I just hope it continues as Dorothy grows older.'

'Aww, it's amazing what being a stepmother has done to you, babe. I never saw it coming.'

'I never saw it coming myself, but she has levelled Jacob out, and she makes me laugh so much. Who would have thought such joy could come from such a tiny package?'

'Have you bloody heard yourself?' Heather beamed.

'I know, I think this is as happy as I have ever been!'

The wedding venue, in the High Rocks forest in Tunbridge Wells, was beautiful in a way that was almost dreamlike. With the evening sun dipping beneath the treeline, a firefly-like swarm of stars had appeared overhead. Jacob stood to attention underneath the arch of wild flowers and looked out at the gathering of friends and family that had come to see them on their special day. He was wearing trousers and a waistcoat in a traditional navy tweed, and a crisp white shirt. A Paul Smith pocket square poked out of his pocket, and his Omega watch was the only other addition to what he hoped was a classic and a lost vintage look. His brother stood with him, wearing identical clothes but hung in a different way. Samuel had always been told, by Jacob no less, that he was the less attractive brother. His style was that of a man who didn't care much for what anyone thought about him. So his shirt was a little less tucked in, and his hair a little less styled. At six feet one inch, Samuel was a touch taller, but they were obviously brothers, and side by side they looked the part.

'Shame Dad didn't get to see you marry the right girl at last,' said Sam, nodding towards their mum, who sat with Dorothy bouncing on her knee.

'Alice was never the wrong girl, mate. I was the wrong guy, though, for sure.'

Samuel put his hand on his brother's back. The violinist started to play, and Samuel leaned in and whispered, 'Damn, son, well done my boy.'

'*It's not so easy loving me,*' sang the female vocalist, who was standing next to the violinist and a man playing an acoustic guitar, whose hair was tied up in a loose bun like a samurai warrior. '*It gets so complicated, all the things you've got to be...*'

As Evan started to walk down the aisle, all eyes were on her elegant and desirable form, perfectly wrapped in a dress that was short at the front but then trailed off to a small train at the rear.

'*Everything's changing but you're the truth, I'm amazed by all your patience, everything I put you through.*'

Jacob's heart froze. He had been so nervous waiting for Alice, as if he knew deep down they weren't right for each other, yet now he felt completely at ease. Just being himself was enough for Evan and Dorothy. He never had to pretend to be anything more.

'*When I'm about to fall, somehow you're always waiting, with your open arms to catch me...*'

Evan stood opposite Jacob. He lifted her veil, to reveal her glossed red lips.

'Ladies and gentlemen, friends and family. We are gathered here today to witness the union of love between Jacob and Evangeline. I believe you have prepared your own vows?' said the minister. 'Evangeline, would you like to go first?'

Evan was shaking but was quickly eased by Jacob, who took her hands within his own.

'There was a time, Jacob Brooking, when I knew I loved you, but I never loved us. All that has changed these past few years. That may be down to a certain young lady.' Evan gave a little wink to Dorothy – a wink that was returned by Dorothy blinking both eyes together tightly. 'Or maybe we just grew into one another. But what I am sure of is you are my best friend, and I have never loved two people more than I love both of you.'

Evan looked once more at Dorothy, but she had disappeared from her grandmother's knee and instead was trying to chase a butterfly down the centre of the aisle, drawing a chorus of delight from the crowd. As she returned her gaze to Jacob, Evan saw the face of a man caught off guard by her honest and, for her at least, articulate declaration of love for Dorothy, on top of her love for him.

With tears starting to well in his eyes, Jacob opened his mouth to speak but felt overwhelmed to do so.

'Baby,' said Evan, giving his hands a gentle shake. 'Just remember the hard part's already done.'

'Evan,' Jacob stuttered. 'I thought I wasn't good enough. Not good enough for my family, for my job, and certainly for anybody that dared to love me. I looked at others to complete me. I looked to run away in hope I might find a piece of me I might like. Then Dotty came along and we found our way and I realised something. I was always enough, and I am a good dad, and I work hard. Let me be a good husband to you, the most beautiful and amazing woman I know, and I promise I won't let you down. You have saved me! I love you with all my heart. You have...'

Jacob paused for a moment, as if waiting for a disapproving voice, as if waiting for the doubt to kick in. It never came, and he finally felt free to say everything that he had always wanted to say.

'You have saved me from myself, and I will show you from today just how much I love you for that.'

Chapter 25:
The Wish and the Girl in the Corner

Song of the day: 'Blackbird'
by Rumer

Autumn 2012

Whitstable, Kent, UK

'Stop it, Dorothy. Can you not see that Mummy is busy?'

Dorothy didn't care that her mum was busy. She was bored and, like most children of that age and of above-average intelligence, needed to be amused by something that would stop her entertaining herself with something inappropriate every time her mum's back was turned. This particular time, she was playing with her mother's paintbrushes. With Alice being the artist she was, they were not cheap, and so Dorothy's misbehaviour was driving her to distraction.

'Baby, those are Mummy's. You have your own, remember? Over here with your books and toys.'

Alice gestured to the little playpen she had set up in the corner of the studio, an art deco version of an Indian tepee. Dorothy still struggled to communicate with her mum the way she communicated with Jacob. She gave Alice a quick look of derision and threw her mother's brushes on the wooden floor before throwing herself into her corner on her belly. Alice let out a frustrated and muffled scream and pulled Dorothy up by her wrists and onto her bottom.

'Baby, please, just help me out and play here whilst I get some work done.'

She instantly regretted snapping at her daughter, but she was so tired. This wasn't a life she had asked for at all.

The little bell above the door chimed like birdsong, announcing the arrival of customers.

'Please, just do this for me,' Alice pleaded with Dorothy before going to greet her new customers. 'Welcome to Le Petit Papillon,' she said proudly, before realising that she knew her customers. 'Mr and Mrs Fitzherbert – I'm sorry, I didn't recognise you for a moment. Not that I could ever forget you in that wonderful coat, Julianne. I wasn't expecting to see you again so soon.'

Mr Pip Fitzherbert, by far the more pretentious and ruder of the two of them, pushed past Alice and pointed at the Viking Bay piece that Alice had painted as an art student at Canterbury University. 'My wife, in all her wisdom, has convinced me to drive all the way back here – despite nearly being on my own driveway an hour ago – so that we can buy this little oil painting of yours. Why she didn't buy it when we were here I just don't know, but here we are.'

'It's a watercolour, Mr Fitzherbert, but of course, I will wrap it for you now. Julianne, have you decided where you might hang –'

Alice was cut off by the catastrophic crash of what she knew to be her current project falling off its easel and smashing on the hard floor, followed closely by the pitter-patter of Dorothy's tiny feet.

'If you could give me a moment,' said Alice, smiling falsely while backing out of the room. This was how Alice's day had begun, and it was how it was to continue.

Alice wasn't a stroppy person. In fact, her very nature emanated a constant state of happiness, as Alice was the very picture of a woman who danced in the rain and sang loudly, not caring who could witness such an event. But as she tucked Dorothy into bed that night, she felt frustrated by the day gone by. A day wasted. The one sale to the Fitzherberts had been the only highlight; her brush had laid not one stroke on her three current projects. Dorothy was already fast asleep, the journey home having knocked her out so much that her grandfather had carried her straight to bed from the car. Alice was glad to have dinner with her folks, especially with the business just taking off and Jacob on his honeymoon with his new practically perfect wife, as Alice had taken to sarcastically calling her. It wasn't always easy for Alice to find time to food-shop, let alone cook a healthy dinner for the both of them, and her mother's attention to Dorothy gave her time to breathe.

Alice looked at her daughter, exhausted from her day of destruction, and wondered how she could sleep so soundly after spending her entire day being so very pestiferous. 'Where did you come from, baby? You are the only thing I don't remember – carrying, birthing or holding you. I remember nothing and I doubt sometimes you are real. Is that why you hate me? I don't know what you want from me, for you still refuse to talk to me, like I am nothing but a nuisance to you, getting in the way of you and your father's fun.' Alice turned on the night light as she backed slowly out of the room, trying not to wake her daughter from her slumber. She closed the door slowly and rested her head on it. 'I mean, how could I possibly compete with your perfect little family over at the Brooking family home?'

She cursed quietly to herself, before a soothing voice intervened.

'You are a great mum,' said Angela Petalow as she handed her daughter a mug of lemon-and-ginger tea. 'Never forget that.'

'Thanks, Mum, but I'm still fairly sure she hates me. I never asked for this, and it scares me the way she looks at me at times.'

Alice walked into her room and sat on her bed, while her mum loitered in the doorway.

'She doesn't hate you, Alice. She is still getting used to you having her more often, that's all.'

Alice looked up into her mum's eyes and spoke honestly. 'All I remember is hating Evan, and then Dorothy was here.'

'My beautiful Alice, look how far you have come since you left hospital. It's hard to hear, I know, but Jacob is a great dad too, and having seen Evan with him and then also with our Dotty, well… I can't argue with the fact that they seem a good fit. Does that take anything away from you, as a woman, as a mother? No! Of course it doesn't. You will find your way in life. You are the most creative and beautiful of all God's creatures, and you will attract those around you that benefit you on a deeper level. That was never our Jacob. Just be you. Dorothy will come around, believe me, my love.' Angela lowered her shoulders and sighed on behalf of her daughter. 'That little poppet is blessed with love in abundance, just like you are. Your father and I are so extremely proud of you.' Angela walked over and kissed her daughter on her brow. 'Get some rest, my love.'

Alice sipped the last of her tea before sliding down under her fleece-lined quilt and curling into a foetal position, one goose-downed pillow held in her tight embrace. Her heart felt heavy, and the drama had taken its toll on her brain's ability to function properly, so she closed her eyes and tried her best to shut off the noise of the day and the bickering mind voices that followed. Then, as everything slowed to a halt, and her mind gave up the fight, nothing came forward, nothing except the silence of the night.

It couldn't have been ten minutes before a crash woke Alice in a startled panic, causing her to almost fall out of bed in a rush to reach her daughter. Dorothy stood next to the spot where her bookcase used to stand and looked first at her mother and then at the smashed lamp on the floor. The glow from Dorothy's comfort lamp picked out the broken porcelain and glass, like a star system scattered across the carpet. Dorothy jumped back onto her bed and defiantly pointed at Mr Blackberry, her regal hare toy, a favourite gift from her father, which lay next to the shattered lamp.

'What have you done, Dorothy? For God's sake, girl, you need to give me a goddamned break.'

Dorothy didn't cry as a result of her mother's outburst. Instead, she lay on her bed and faced the wall.

'You can turn your back to me all you want, Miss Brooking, but I tell you now that you are going to change your attitude or you can go and live with your bloody father from the minute he returns, and you can stay there until you realise just how easy you had it here.'

Alice picked up every shard of anything that had the potential to hurt her daughter's delicate feet and stood the bookcase up with a rage-fuelled burst of strength. She replaced the books one by one before throwing Mr Blackberry on the bed next to a sulking Dorothy. 'Can I go to sleep now, Your Majesty? Is that OK?'

Dorothy didn't respond and cared little for her mother's sarcasm, leaving Alice to close the door behind her and rest her brow once more on its painted wood.

'I didn't ask for this. Why can't you just leave me alone!' Alice cried with a flushed red face.

As you wish, said the creature in the hallway mirror, which looked like Alice, but sounded like Thomas Levit.

Chapter 26:

I Move the Stars for No One

Song of the day: 'Life on Mars?'
by David Bowie

Autumn 2012

Canterbury, Kent, UK

Rain lashed hard against the windowpane, waking Alice up from a dream of beautiful calm. She had been walking through a field of sunflowers, with the sun itself baking down on the ground, as she playfully chased a butterfly while skipping to the song of chirping birds and busy crickets.

WHAT'S WRONG, ALICE? called the creature from the reflection in the window. Its form was barely visible, but somehow the water pounding against it was creating a silhouette. It had been years since Alice had kept a mirror in her bedroom, but somehow her demon self always found a way to show its face and communicate its venom, be it a rainy window or a make-up mirror.

Dorothy, check Dorothy. Alice looked at her phone to assess the time. One o'clock was a good time – if all was well and the creature left her alone, then another six hours' sleep wasn't beyond the realms of possibility. She slid out of bed and onto the cold and uninviting floor while blindly fumbling for her slippers. The rain's beat became more aggressive and overpowered all of Alice's other senses as she staggered blindly in the dark, yawning and stretching all the way to Dorothy's room. She went to open Dorothy's door, but the darkness betrayed her, as it was already wide open. Alice rushed over to Dorothy's bed to make sure all was well. She had felt guilty all night for the falling-out during the day. Whatever was wrong with their relationship, Alice was fairly sure it wasn't the fault of her nearly five-year-old daughter. She pulled the quilt back from the heap of pillows and was hit instantly with the dread she had feared the most.

As you wished, my child

Alice staggered back. *Dad, she will be with Dad.* Seeking sanctuary with the big bear was something Alice herself had done throughout her childhood, especially during violent storms. She turned to go and check but was stopped abruptly by a lancing pain deep within her foot. The pain was so intense that it brought her tumbling to her knees. Alice muffled her scream between pursed lips. She realised she couldn't take her slipper off to look at the source of the pain, as a shard of glass from the shattered lamp had pierced the bottom of her heel, pinning her plush shoe to her flesh. 'Fuck, fuck, fuck,' Alice cursed quietly while biting down on her lip to avoid waking the whole house up. 'Jesus, Alice, you can do this,' she said. She gripped the glass dagger between her two fingers.

Does it hurt?

Alice looked to her right and saw her demon self in Dorothy's mirrored wardrobe. For once, it wasn't wearing identical clothes. Instead, it wore a white communion dress that looked far too small for someone or something of Alice's size. It was just like... No, it *was* Dorothy's communion dress.

Does it hurt? the creature repeated. It licked its lips and pressed its filthy blood-stained hands against the mirror's glass front, as if trapped in a transparent cell.

Alice ignored the creature and wrenched the shard out with a suppressed yelp. 'I'm not letting you toy with me, creature.' She pulled herself up and hobbled to the door, leaving a bloody footprint behind her with every step of her right foot.

'Mum, Dad, are you awake?'

Alice didn't wait for a reply. She turned the handle to her parents' bedroom door. On the other side, she found everything she had ever feared. No roof sheltered the decaying corpses of her parents, only a hellish, blood-red sky; no carpet lay beneath her feet, only hard stone and hot volcanic ash. Her parents, flayed and desiccated, were lying on their bed, side by side and hand in hand. Yet as Alice battled herself, convincing herself with every look that none of this could be real, a worse sight caught her eye. The sky filled with rapacious black-winged creatures, too large to be birds. Each one shrieked and clawed for aerial dominance over the blood heaven, a dance that saw blood shed by razor-sharp talons and jagged-edged beaks. When Alice screamed at the horror unfolding in front of her, the harpies' focus turned to her, and in that moment Alice realised that behind the sharp beaks of the nightmare creatures were deformed and black-eyed versions of every girl who had ever bullied her at school. With renewed hunger and wanton desire, the beasts swooped down one by one to devour Alice as they had done her parents.

Alice turned to leave the room, but the door she had entered was gone. In its place was the same barren stone landscape that surrounded her. Black stone and a blood-red sky were her everything now. As she started to run, a quick glance over her shoulder told her that her parents' corpses had disappeared. She ran. She ran until she could feel the bile rising in her throat. Her slippers were torn off by the jagged rock. She kept going, kept on running, until the skin on her feet was shredded. The demonic harpies, easily the size of a Rottweiler and with the harrowed and tortured faces of all of her oppressors, ripped her nightdress from her body and took turns in attempting to tear the flesh from her shoulders and back. As Alice rounded a larger slab of obsidian slate that ran down a slope dangerously steep to a woman running so fast, she ran shoulder-first into the front door of a large detached house that had seemingly come out of nowhere. Alice burst through the red oak door, slamming it behind her and pulling across an archaic iron bolt as a means of defence. She didn't know if these creatures knew how to open a door, but as she slid to the floor to tend her bloodied and blackened feet, she realised she didn't care, because this couldn't be real. It couldn't be… *Could it?*

Three of the closest harpies slammed into the door with sickening thuds as Alice pushed up onto her haunches and added her weight to it to keep it secure. The creatures shrieked and snapped with fang-filled beaks.

'Where am I?' said Alice as she got herself up to her feet.

You are where you wanted to be, Alice, said her demon self as it entered the room from an arched entrance that led to a kitchen that looked more like a torture chamber.

'You're not real, bitch,' said Alice confidently. 'I'm scared, I'm hurt, but I'm not stupid. You have brought me to your false reality far too many times.'

Do I look like a reflection in your mirror to you this time? I have told you where you are – exactly where you wanted to be. Away from your bastard child… She will be happier with her "better" parents anyway

'THAT'S NOT WHAT I WANTED, AND YOU KNOW IT… WHERE IS SHE?'

Alice took a step towards her dark reflection. Her demon self moved with unnatural form and almost supernatural speed, pinning Alice by the throat as its clawed hand clasped her neck, forcing air and blood to spurt out of her mouth.

I move the stars for no one, Alice, and yet here you are, demanding from me, screaming at me, wanting FROM ME…

The creature's clawed digits punctured her throat, drawing yet more blood as it brought its face to hers. Its rotten teeth were black and yellow, with pieces of rotting flesh in every crevice. The creature's torn skin was almost translucent, and Alice could have sworn that there were insects writhing underneath the thin layer of flesh used to bind this form together.

What right do you have to ask anything of me? You wanted peace from the child that you deem not your own. I have brought it, and now you see fit to complain about that, as if I should somehow care what you want

The creature's grip increased, and Alice pulled on its wrists to prevent her imminent choking, but as her attempts only seemed to pull away rotting flesh from its arms, she soon gave up and let the darkness take over.

Not yet, said the creature.

With a snap of its wrist and a turn of its deformed body, it threw Alice across the room, towards the archway, where she smashed hard against the wall. She fought to stay conscious, air flooding her empty lungs.

You will never escape me; you are just a vessel of my omnipotent form

Alice scrambled into the kitchen on all fours, bloodying her knees as she went. She pulled herself up eventually and glanced through the rear window to see the harpies picking at a corpse at the rear of the house. A creature with the face of Chloe Durby – one of her tormentors from her school days – plucked an eye from the corpse with its jagged beak, swallowing it down as it craned its neck to the sky. Petrified, Alice spun around to face her demon self as it followed her into the kitchen, almost climbing the unit behind her to escape its gaze.

You ungrateful whore

'You're not real,' screamed Alice. She fumbled for and then gripped a large, rusty, curved knife, which resembled a garden sickle rather than any kitchen blade. Brandishing it above her head like a scorpion, she said once more, 'You're not real.'

Bless you, you pathetic piece of shit. You actually think you can hurt me. I told you before, I will eat your soul and then your precious daughter's after that

'NO!' screamed Alice, as she brought the blade down towards an on-rushing blur of hatred in physical form, one whose mouth had opened unnaturally wide to expose the venom-toothed fangs among the rotten remains of its normal teeth. Alice brought the blade down in an arc that cleaved the creature's face in two. Its eyes fell apart by a few inches, as if the creature was losing its mask. Even its tongue was split like that of a serpent, yet the creature still smiled as its two tongues whipped about independently.

You can't hurt me, child, but I will embrace your fight, for I relish the pain and the flood of human sensations that come with it

Its claws sunk into Alice's flesh again. It gripped her tightly by the arms to stop her from launching another attack, and then opened its mouth wide like a boa constrictor, burying its teeth into Alice's shoulder and neck.

Yet Alice didn't move, didn't flinch and didn't make a sound.

Have you given up? See, I knew you wanted it. Why else would you stop fighting me?

Alice smiled, and that smile increased despite the dozen puncture marks across her shoulder and neckline that oozed blood and venom.

'Thomas,' said Alice. 'I can see your face beneath my own.'

The creature withdrew and held its hands up to its falling mask. Thomas Levit was staring back at Alice. His face beneath the monster's was perfect, clean and unbroken.

'You have no power over me, Thomas, and if you ever did – well, not anymore!'

The creature screamed and lunged at her, sinking its teeth into her battered body, but again Alice didn't react.

'You have no power over me,' Alice said proudly, as she closed her eyes and clenched her fists. 'YOU HAVE NO POWER OVER ME!!!'

Alice opened her eyes to find herself sitting upright in her bed. She was drenched in sweat and was fairly sure she had wet herself, but she was safe, and this was real, she could feel it.

'Mummy.' Dorothy was at the door.

'What's wrong, poppet?' said Alice, smiling at her beautiful daughter, the mirror of her younger self.

'Mummy, I had a bad dream,' said a tear-filled Dorothy, holding tightly onto Mr Blackberry.

'Go and get into bed, baby, whilst I quickly go and wash. And then how about I come and snuggle in your bed?'

'OK, Mum.'

With a pitter-patter of her tiny feet, Dorothy ran back to her room.

Alice took a deep breath and stepped into her en suite shower.

As the hot water ran over her body, her reflection in the bathroom mirror continued to flicker between her own and that of the man who had raped her. But she couldn't care less, and as she wrapped herself in a towel, she ran her hand over the moisture-covered mirror. Only her face remained.

'I've got you now, you bastard,' she said confidently. 'You have no power over me.'

Chapter 27:Godfather Death

Song of the day: 'The Butterfly Collector' by The Jam

Winter 2012

St Martin's Hospital, Kent, UK

'I can't let you stay in there for long,' said Sister Bonnie with absolute authority.

'I know, Bon,' answered Alice with false confidence. 'It's just something I have to do.'

'I get that, my treasure, I really do. Just get from this what you need and then leave it all behind in that room with him. Do you hear me, Miss Alice?'

Alice nodded slowly but in full agreement. She placed her hand on the door and slowly pushed through with a resolute strength she was eager to show through the entirety of the coming conflict, but as she stepped into the room, the wind was taken from her sails almost immediately. Thomas Levit had been a hard man to find. She had visited all his old teammates back at Canterbury RFC – the ones that her father still had connections with, at any rate – but no one had seen him in years. She had hit social media hard in the hope that his name would pop up in certain circles, and yet again, nothing had cropped up. His whereabouts had come, eventually, from a peculiar avenue. She'd gone to see Bonnie, and they'd gone for an overpriced hospital-grade sandwich in the cafeteria. Alice overheard a group of bitching nurses, who were sitting at the next table, talking about him.

She didn't find out why Thomas was at St Martin's until she stood at the end of his bed.

Thomas Nathaniel Levit, diagnosis: Glioblastoma Multiforme Grade IV astrocytoma. Alice didn't understand what this meant. Treatment: best supportive care. Ward Notes: TLC Two Hourly Turns. No OBS necessary. Nurse to change syringe driver 10/12/12. One of the nurses told her it was as severe a brain tumour as they had ever seen at Canterbury Oncology.

'No less than you deserve, Thomas.' Alice spoke gently, looking at his frail body and replacing the clipboard. Tubes and wires were coming out of every orifice on his body, some natural, others man-made. A machine designed with the sole purpose of keeping him breathing was sat next to him, permanently humming and clicking, and two drips seemed to be doing their very best to keep the reaper at bay.

Thomas looked up. Alice wasn't sure if he recognised her or not. The hums, whirs and clicks kept the room from being silent, if not awkward, and Alice knew that if death did exist as an entity, then he was most definitely sitting at the head of Thomas Levit's bed.

Alice took her time to soak up the reality of the situation that faced her. She had played this confrontation out in her head so many times with every possible scenario, yet this she had not considered. Thomas was gaunt, far too weak to even raise a murmur to communicate with Alice, and that suited her just fine, or so she thought at first. His sunken eyes looked full of fear – maybe the fear of a man who envisaged his victim getting revenge. Alice wasn't here to kill him, though; she was here to win back her life. She walked around the bed and perched on the edge of his mattress, taking his wrist in her hands to prove, both to Thomas and herself, that she was in control of the situation. Noticing that she could close a very loose loop about his wrist with little effort, she dropped the limp appendage back to the bed with a smile.

'It's been a while,' said Alice. She looked straight into his black-ringed eyes – something she had promised herself she would do. 'I won't beat around the bush. I had to tell you in no uncertain terms that I hate you. I hate you for what you did to me. For not even realising the magnitude of what you did to me, and for the endless suffering you have put me through since that day, just because you needed to give your ego a boost. And then for letting that damage affect my relationship with my daughter.' Alice was unrelenting and focused in her verbal tirade. 'I hate you because as you lie there dying in front of me, you probably see yourself as the victim here.' Alice rose defiantly to her feet and drew herself closer to his almost skeletal face. 'But what I hate the most, Thomas "fucking captain of the rugby team" Levit, is that you are so pathetic right now, so weak, that you cannot even find the strength to come up with some bullshit excuse for your crimes.'

Alice turned her back to him, and her navy-blue dress swung behind her like a cape. The hum and whir of the machines was matched by the click of her heels as she strode away from him. She stopped briefly in the door, without turning about, as she didn't need to face him anymore. 'One last thing before I go. The nurses have told me you have barely any time left and that I am your first visitor in months. So, I hope you enjoy the irony that I might well be the last person you see from outside the hospital walls.' Alice paused to catch both the moment and her breath. 'Goodbye, Thomas. You won't see me again. And believe me when I say that I won't be seeing you either.'

Thomas Levit died 48 hours later, alone in his hospital bed, with only the hums, clicks and whirs of the machines for company. He hadn't recognised the girl that had visited him days before, for she was just one of many people he had surely hurt over the years. She'd had her life turned upside down by this monster of a man, who looked at Alice as just another face. The visit, though, had reminded him of the direction that the reaper would lead him, and Thomas Levit, with little show of the violence he had become renowned for, cried in fear until his heart stopped, the beeps turned to a flat-lined pitch, and the shadow of death took him away.

Chapter 28: Dear Jacob

Song of the day: 'The Pebble and the Boy' by Paul Weller

Spring 2013

Whitstable, Kent, UK

The task was simple: clear the air and make things right. With the shop thriving in a way her false reality had seemed to predict all too accurately and Dorothy finding a place by her mother's side at last, it had become more apparent that her life was back on track and that actually having her best friend back on board would benefit both her own life and Dorothy's.

He seemed happy now, and it pleased Alice to see him so settled, as it was something she had never seen before. He was great with Dorothy too. In fact, he doted on her so much that Alice couldn't believe his devotion at times. Yes, they could be friends; she was sure of it. In fact, despite his good looks seeming to only get better with age, Alice had found herself not looking at him that way anymore. She pondered for a moment if that was down to Evan's touch. Maybe that was why she could look at his handsome face and appreciate it the way she would a friend's. Jacob just didn't tick those boxes for her anymore. He and Evan looked more suited, anyway. She had seen them out shopping one day at the Ashford outlet in the summer and had resisted announcing her presence, choosing instead to awkwardly stalk them for ten minutes to get the measure of their relationship. They had looked like one of those magazine couples that you love to hate for being a little too perfect. From the safety of a Starbucks window seat, she had watched Jacob roll with laughter as Evan tried to play-fight with him. She had never seen him laugh so loud, never seen him so carefree. In Evan she had noticed a change, too. Since they had worked together at the restaurant, Evan had gone for a more natural look, and it surprised Alice just how stunning she was naturally, and more secure within herself. With true love apparently in her heart, that false confidence had fallen away. Alice doubted she could ever be friends with Evan or even come close to forgiving her, but it was a good thing they were happy, as it made Dotty happy. Dotty adored Evan and her dad, which drove Alice mad with jealousy, even if she was truly grateful for it.

Alice dropped the letter into the postbox and instantly felt a little lighter on her feet. *Maybe this was overdue*, she thought as she climbed onto her vintage push bike, the wicker basket on the front filled with flowers to decorate Le Petit Papillon.

Onwards and upwards, Alice Marie Petalow, onwards and upwards.

Dearest Jacob

Where do I begin to tell my first true love that I am happy for him, and that I want to be free of the restraints that have kept him from being my best friend these past few years, years that to be fair have not been kind to me? I guess I'll start by saying that you can read this freely knowing that this is not an attack. After all, I know how your mind works. I wanted to thank you and Evan (yes, you read that right, feel free to photograph that and send it to my father) for everything you do for our Dorothy. You are a better dad than I ever could have wished for you to be, and our daughter worships the pair of you. Thank you for finding a focus with her that I never knew you possessed.

Which brings me to this... I don't hate you, Jay. In fact, I don't even hate Evan. Let's be clear on one thing, I am not absolving either of you of the choices you made when we were together. But I do realise now that you had no idea what was going on in my head during the early years of our relationship, and maybe one day when we are old and you are grey, and we are down at Tankerton seafront chatting away like two old hands, sat on a bench because the walk is too much for us, and Evan is long gone from a Botox overdose (joke), well, maybe then I'll tell you what I was going through. But for now, just know that although you were a giant dick, my suicide attempt was nothing to do with you. That being said, you shouldn't have kept your condition from me for so long. It was that lack of communication that ultimately ruined us – that and the simple fact that you shouldn't have married me if you had feelings for anyone else. Let alone the daughter of our therapist (I know, right – you should have seen my face).

I don't want to dig up the past, though, and so I'll say no more and we can move forward. I just felt with the conclusion of my therapy last week – a journey that has taken me over ten years, if you can believe it – maybe it was time we drew a line under our past. I know you struggle to always get to Dotty on time in the week, so I thought we could move things about a little, as I'm now settled in the apartment above the studio. So if you wanted to pick Dotty up direct from me rather than driving into Canterbury, you will save yourself 40 minutes in traffic, and although my coffee isn't as good as my mum's, it will be good to catch up once or twice a week.

We will never be best friends, you and I, and Evan will never share a bottle of wine with me on a summer's night, but I do think we are due some peace in our lives, and honestly I see this as the way forward.

I am incredibly proud of who you have become, Jay. Your father would be too.

Pebble xxx

Chapter 29: Dear Alice

Song of the day: 'Something' by The Beatles

Spring 2013

Faversham, Kent, UK

To my Dearest ~~Alice Pebble~~ Alice

Words cannot explain the gratitude I feel for your kindness, a trait in you that I have never deserved to see. You are right in what you say, communication was never our forte and has never been my strong point at all. When I needed to talk to you I couldn't, and when you needed me to listen, I wasn't there. It was a problem throughout our relationship that I forever felt incapable of being the man that you deserved, and in reading your letter that has once again been proved true, I am reminded once more just how lucky I am to have you in my life in any capacity whatsoever. I am touched by your words and your endless empathy for those who wrong you. And you were right, if I had spoken to you of my demons, of my insecurities, then things would have been different, I am sure. I certainly believe that had I spent more time listening to your pain rather than battling that constant chip on my shoulder, well, maybe I could have lightened your load a little. It took me some time to realise that my biggest failing to you was not as a husband, but as your friend, a friend born all those years before on those

Tankerton slopes you speak about so fondly. So, with that said, I am truly sorry, Alice, for not being the friend I should have been.

You are a great mum, a fantastic daughter, and seeing you flourish as a businesswoman is such a wonderful thing that I am filled with pride.

I've spoken to Evan and she's moved by your words. She understands that you will never be friends, but she wants you to know she doesn't see you as an enemy, in fact she never has been.

Thank you for showing me a respect I'm sure I don't deserve.

Thank you for being the influence our daughter needs.

Thank you for being the most colourful and unique pebble on my Plutonian shore.

All my love, Jacob x

Jacob patted the letter, as if to wish it a safe journey, and dropped it into the postbox. *Long overdue*, he thought. He had believed Alice to be the answer to all his problems, yet he saw now that he had always been enough on his own. That's how he knew that his love for Evan was real, because he had never needed her; he just felt happier when she was by his side. Alice had enabled his bad behaviour for far too long, and he had repaid her with nothing but misery. He didn't deserve her friendship, but he was extremely glad that he had it.

Chapter 30: Glad Rags

Song of the day: 'I Hate Love Songs' by Kelsea Ballerini

Summer 2013

Ramsgate, Kent, UK

Alice wasn't blown away by the idea of tonight. Speed dating had been her best friend Holly's idea; it certainly wasn't something she would have forced on herself. 'We can do it together,' Holly had said. 'We don't do anything anymore. You might as well still be in that bloody coma.'

Alice pulled up at the venue and slipped on her scarlet-red stiletto heels – to drive in them would surely have been a death sentence. She stepped out of the car and onto the cobbles, reset the fall of her strappy white top as it dropped over her curves, and pulled her phone out of her suede clutch bag.

There was a text from Holly:

Alice, I'm not coming. This was all a ruse to get you dating again. So get your ass in there, as I've paid your fee already and I'm tired of you being a loser on your own every night. You're a MILF now, don't forget. Go work that little ass of yours.

The text was frustrating, but not out of the blue. Alice had suspected foul play when her illustrious and bubbly friend had refused the opportunity to get ready together with a few bottles of wine and a shared taxi. *Right, Pebble, you've got this.* She stepped through the hotel doors. With her hair up in a tight auburn bun, she looked the part of the alpha female, even if she didn't feel anywhere near as confident as the image she was projecting.

BZZZZZZZZZ

The buzzer sounded and the first potential knight in shining armour sat down in front of Alice. Already bored by the dull surroundings, she wished she was outside, sketching the seafront.

'I'm Robert, but you can call me "the boy", 'cause my friends think I'm the man. I know, silly right? Although I do have quite a solid investment portfolio – I imagine that's why they gave me the moniker. So, it's OK here… The Stella seems cheap enough and the fanny is packed in tightly. You know what, though, I think you and me are a notch above the rest. How about we just head off, leave these suckers behind, am I right? No? OK. So what is it you do for a living, Alice, other than day trips to wonderland – you know, because of your name. I reckon you're a secretary, you look like a secretary. I have my own PA. It's like having a wife at work. She makes me coffee and empties my trash bin. Only difference is I don't have to bang her fat ass.'

The fat, balding ginger man in front of Alice didn't stop for breath from the second he sat down, and the sound of the buzzer was a sweet release.

'Hi, Alice. My name's Evan.'

Alice laughed out loud and refused to talk for the duration of the three minutes of allotted time, other than to clarify that she couldn't date a man with the same name as the woman who stole her husband.

'Hello, red,' said the next man, clearly a vegan, his hemp shoes giving it away far too easily. Keith was a miserable man of short stature and clearly stoned. Kieran didn't seem to have a brain cell in his head and fidgeted to such a degree that Alice presumed he had either ADHD or a crack addiction. Gregory wore a pair of old school shoes, along with trousers, a shirt, a tie and a baseball cap, and he smelled of wet dog and cheap lager. The quality didn't pick up for the remainder of the hour, and Alice ticked no boxes to meet any of them again. *You are so much more than this,* Alice told herself as she prepared to leave.

Suddenly, a gentle hand took the loop of her arm and guided her to the door.

'Just keep walking.' The petite girl who had been sitting next to Alice had a thick Tennessee accent. 'The crack addict was ready to make another pass at you.'

They fell into the street giggling, full of the joy that freedom had given them from the dour confines of such a grotty hotel.

'I'm Poppy, and I think you and I deserve a proper drink. That sound good, sugar?'

She looked like a curvy Winona Ryder; Alice was a little jealous of her shape. 'A drink sounds great, but let's move quick before the horde follows us out.'

They joined arms once more and skipped down the back streets until they found a wine bar more suited to the women they were.

'So, you're from Tennessee, but live in Kansas,' said Alice, already on her second glass of wine. Getting a hotel looked ever more likely.

Poppy smiled, running her fingers through her dark, pixie-cut hair. The colour was almost replicated in her hazel eyes, which had a haunting depth.

'That is correct, sugar,' she said, sipping on a botanical gin cocktail that Alice had recommended. 'I still can't believe this isn't a thing in the States.'

'What is it you do for a living?'

'I am, for my sins, an art buyer for a gallery back home. I get to travel all over the world and look at the most beautiful paintings. I majored in fine art at the University of San Francisco and never looked back.' Poppy put her hand on Alice's thigh. 'And you are an artist yourself.'

'What makes you say that?' gasped Alice.

'Because I just spent an hour listening to the most interesting person in the room tell men what she does for a living and then reject the hell out of all their dumb asses, and I can't blame you at all.' Poppy's southern drawl was becoming heavier with each passing drink. 'I mean, I'm gay, and even I could see there were slim pickings on that BBQ.'

'OK, I'm open-minded, I probably could have guessed gay if I hadn't seen you in there with me. So what was that about? Or do you just go to pick up demoralised chicks?' Alice giggled and gave her a nudge of the shoulder.

'Oh, you think that's what I was doing? Because, girl, you looked empowered, not demoralised. I like to people-watch and hear bullshit stories. I won't lie, I'm a bit of a social butterfly, and that seemed the only place to be in this smelly harbour town.'

There was something so refreshing about Poppy's company, and Alice was revelling in it.

'Do you know what we should do now, honey pie?' said Alice in a mock accent that failed to mimic her counterpart with any authenticity.

'Hit me, sugar plum,' Poppy responded in a much more successful cockney accent. 'And don't give me no twaddle.'

Alice downed her wine and offered her hand as she slid out of the booth. 'Let's go dancing.'

'Dancing?'

'Dancing,' reiterated an energetic Alice.

Poppy smiled and took her hand, and they ran through the streets of the small fishing town until they found a place to call their own.

Alice woke up at about 2 a.m. to her phone vibrating across the glass bedside unit. Its sound was like a jackhammer to her head, and it woke her with a fright as she tried to get her bearings in a room she didn't recognise. She fumbled for her phone. Poppy was passed out cold, still fully dressed and holding onto a bottle of water as if it was the only thing that could save her from the upcoming hangover. *Mum? What does she want at this time?* thought Alice while trying to find her equilibrium.

'Mum... What's wrong?'

Chapter 31: Stay

Song of the day: 'Stay' by Thirty Seconds to Mars

Summer 2013

Queen Elizabeth Hospital, Margate, Kent, UK

Evan watched a focused John Petalow stalk the halls of Queen Elizabeth Hospital like a lion caged in a space only twice its size. He was calm enough, yet, like a dormant volcano, it paid to give him some space. She had never been formally introduced to John when she had managed the restaurant floor at the Gallantry. As the owner of the Mile End fish market, John had been sighted often enough, as he ran through fish prices with Matt or Jay over coffee, but Evan had only ever exchanged greetings with him.

Angela had been very welcoming; it had taken Evan completely off guard when Alice's mum had wrapped her arms around her before placing a hand gently on her shoulder and proclaiming that she could see what all the fuss was about. Evan couldn't believe how much Dorothy and Alice looked like her.

Jacob hadn't said much since the news had come in of Dorothy's ruptured appendix. Full dad mode had kicked in and he'd been unnervingly proactive in packing some clothes and toys for her and putting them in the car. But the journey to the hospital had been deathly quiet. Jacob had a need for control that often left him anxious about being a passenger in any capacity; whether in a car or a conversation, he had to be in the driving seat. But he had accepted her offer to drive without a fight and had spent the journey looking up at the stars through the panoramic glass roof of the car.

She drew his hand up to her lips and gave it the slightest squeeze before gently pressing her lips against the back of it.

'I love you,' said Jacob without looking at his attentive wife. 'She's going to be OK, right?'

Evan pulled his gaze around to hers with the deft touch of her painted nails. 'This is a procedure the surgeons have done a thousand times before, and you know what a fighter our little lady is.'

Jacob took heart in Evan's words, before rising to his feet to greet a frantic Alice, who burst through the door like a tempest.

'Jay, what's going on?'

'Appendix is being taken out as we speak. It hasn't burst, but it was beginning to rupture, and this was the only action to prevent a serious problem. The surgeon is the best in Kent by all accounts, and Bonnie has already been on the phone to make sure they are doing everything to the letter.'

Jacob's words were strong and honest, and Alice relaxed enough to start saying hello to everyone, wrapping her arms first around her mum and then her lumbering beast of a father. Evan got a nod of recognition that she returned with a raised hand. Evan had never really liked Alice, but the poor girl hadn't had it easy, and even she had to admit that Alice probably had more reason to dislike her than the other way around.

'I've got to go and stretch my legs, baby.' Jacob bent down and kissed Evan on the top of her head. 'Can you keep an eye on things here?'

'Are you sure you don't need the company?' Evan was a little anxious at the prospect of being left alone with the Petalows.

'No, I'll be OK,' said Jacob, missing the reasoning for Evan asking in the first place. 'I won't be long, I promise.'

He slipped out of the door at the back of the room, opposite the entrance Alice had entered, and fell against the wall on the other side. *What the hell is going on?* he thought as the whole hospital moved as if he was on a ship sailing rough seas.

Jacob pulled himself up the staircase, feeling as though he had been heavily sedated. The hall was spinning. As he pulled himself in front of the top-floor fire escape, it became apparent that his delusion of sea sickness was misinformed. This was no delusion. Jacob pushed through into the open air and was hit by a wave of gigantic proportions. Salt, sand and seaweed hit him like a boxing glove as he was thrown to the deck. *The deck? Where am I? No… It can't be…*

Chapter 32: The Kraken and Her

Song of the day: 'Paint it Black' by The Rolling Stones

Summer 2013

Queen Elizabeth Hospital, Margate, Kent, UK

Moonlight alone illuminated the deck of the *Summer Breeze*, which was being thrown violently around by a storm all too familiar to him. He knew this place well. The smell of the varnished maple deck and the icy-cold seawater that lashed it with every throw of oceanic anger could not hide the sense of anguish that Jacob felt at being back here. He had nearly died here, painfully and slowly, and the motion of the ship rocking violently sent his trauma-filled heart into relapse.

Jacob stepped back towards the fire escape but paused as he heard a familiar sound approaching from behind. The creature was huge and easily filled the corridor with its mass of wet, leathery tentacles, which, one by one, slapped the floor aggressively as it pulled itself towards Jacob at a speed that belied its size and girth. A giant maw sat at its centre, and it had two obsidian eyes that were the very colour of emptiness.

Did you think that you had escaped me, boy?

The creature's voice was clear in Jacob's head, and yet when the kraken opened its beak to voice the words that Jacob could hear transmitted to him, a high-pitched scream, like nails on a blackboard, cut through his soul.

'YOU ARE NOT REAL; YOU NEVER HAVE BEEN,' Jacob screamed above the noise of the screeching creature, howling wind and thunderous waves.

Then why, pray tell, are you backing away from me as though scared? If I am not a real entity, then surely you could let me close my jaws around you, as I have done so many times before

'I'm a fool, Ahab, my old friend, but I am no idiot. Do you hear me?' Jacob backed into the brass railing that surrounded the deck. 'What you do to me I know is far from real; it is no more real than any dream within a dream. But I know that what I dream with you tends to have rather bloody and violent repercussions for me on the floor of the hospital hallway or wherever I actually am.' Jacob climbed over the railing and felt the cold, hard lash of the furious ocean on his back.

You won't jump, Jacob! You have never had the heart to escape me. After all, who are you without me? You with your happy little family, with your girls. You will get bored, you always do, and then you will be all alone without me by your side

Jacob smiled, knowing that he had the strength inside to beat the creature once and for all. No fear shackled him, no power bound him. He was, as he had always been, free to make his own choices.

He let go of the railing just as a barbed tentacle wrapped itself around his forearm. Three loops of viscous black mass looped around his limb like a boa constrictor taking the life of a young deer, and as Jacob resisted the creature's pull, its beak snapping viciously at him, he took a moment to stare into the eyes of his tormentor one last time, so he could truly see his nemesis in this game of real life and false death.

Alice watched Evan get up to follow her beloved husband not two minutes after he had left, bitter that Evan had been sitting here playing happy families with her parents while she was stuck in traffic. *Who does she think she is?* was voiced over and again within the depths of Alice's overthinking mind.

Before she had the calmness and soundness of mind to convince herself to do otherwise, she was on her feet and chasing Evan up the staircase in angry pursuit. *She has no right to be here, none at all. She's not my family or Dorothy's, and we don't need her here.* Alice's lungs burned as she raced to find her. Turning into the hall, she saw Evan go through the fire escape at the end of the ward. A crowd of onlookers were frantically gesturing between them. *First Thomas, then you. You need to be dealt with. You need to hear my voice, all my voices, as I reprimand you for stepping into mine and Jacob's world.* Alice let the air return to her lungs as she recovered her composure. *I'll show you that I am neither meek nor the quiet little butterfly that you believe me to be.* Alice pushed aside the few people blocking the fire escape with a forceful, no-nonsense apology.

Evan had a tight hold of Jacob, who was standing on the wrong side of the security fence that lined the roof of the five-storey hospital. His eyes were vacant, in a place that Alice had seen him visit many times before. *You know this, Alice, he doesn't come back from this for hours, his psychosis is too deep. It always was...*

'Evan, baby, where am I?' said Jacob, grabbing the railing with his free hand.

'I've got you, my love. Don't rush. Just slowly step over onto this side.'

Evan stroked his face and never broke eye contact. He trusted her with his life, and she knew what to do in situations like this, for she knew her Jacob. As he stepped over the low fence and fell into her arms, she instantly sunk down to the ground with him and cradled his head against her breast.

'I don't know what happened,' said Jacob as floods of tears erupted from his red eyes.

'Yes, you do.' Evan caressed and kissed his head. 'You were scared for our Dorothy, and you let your demon back in for a moment. And that's OK.'

Evan kissed his brow and then took his hands to help him up.

'It's always OK to be scared, but I've got you, and we have got this. Together,' said Evan, pulling Jacob to his feet with a groan.

'Thank you, my love.' Jacob, with inconsolable tears still

running down his face, wrapped his arms around her tightly. 'Together.'

Alice watched them link their fingers into a tight embrace as they headed off the roof.

'Evan, I… I hope you are both OK,' said Alice, marvelling at the unison between them.

'Thank you, Alice,' said Evan with the smallest of smiles. 'Shall we go get some coffee?'

'Coffee sounds… Frankly, it sounds great.' Alice let them past and followed closely behind. *You never pulled him round that quickly. I guess it must be love,* she thought gladly, but as she witnessed the bond between Jacob and Evan grow, it was only understanding that she gained. She couldn't forgive them. Deep down inside her, in the place where the demon Alice slept, she thought only of hurting them both like she had been hurt.

Chapter 33: The Light Between Us

Song of the day: 'Big Things Going Down' by Dan Patlansky

Spring 2014

Reculver, Kent, UK

'You've sold the restaurant?' said Evan as she turned onto the coastal road that led down to the Reculver seafront. 'YOU? You who loves his restaurant?'

Jacob smiled in a way that would have told anyone who looked at him that he was really pleased with himself. 'Sold it.'

'What is going on here, and why the hell am I driving? You never let me drive, and now you're acting more suspicious than a puppy sitting next to a carpet turd.' Despite wanting to know what was going on, Evan was in good cheer. She liked seeing Jacob enjoy his day, even if it was a mischievous game of his, which kept drawing little smiles from his lips.

It felt like the first day of summer. The top was down on Evan's Mazda, and they could feel their skin starting to burn in the heat.

'You are driving because I, good lady, am drunk,' Jacob joked theatrically. 'Well, maybe not drunk, but I've had a few with Matt to say goodbye and all that jazz. And nothing's going on. You really have to stop being so paranoid.' Jacob was giggling to himself like a prepubescent schoolboy now, which only encouraged Evan to press harder.

'OK, smart arse. If you are going to play this game, I guess I'll start playing you at it. So… how much have you sold the restaurant for?'

Jacob replied as if he was informally reading the price of West Ham United's latest signing in the Saturday paper. 'Two point six million.'

Evan nearly ran into a hedge as the seafront came into view. 'Two point six million *pounds*?'

'I think it's pounds. I mean, I just presumed it would be,' joked Jacob with a pretend hiccup to boot, which drew a slap across his thigh – an action he used as a means to interlock their fingers. 'I love you so much,' he said, kissing the back of her hand. 'I tell you what, park over by this lighthouse and tell me what happened with your visit to your mum's this morning, and then maybe, just maybe, I'll tell you what's going on.'

That morning

Rat-a-tat-tat.

Evan knocked hard on her mother's door. It came across as angry, which wasn't her intention at all. In fact, the opposite might have been closer to the truth. Evan was here to make things right, to make things like they had been before. *Well, not as before,* she thought, because before was rubbish too.

Evan's mother was a curious woman, a woman of pure focus and unbridled drive, ever the psychologist, unable to switch off and just be a mother.

While she wanted to come across as strong and confident, Evan didn't dare use her own key to let herself in. After all these years, there was no guarantee it would work anyway. In actual fact, had her mother's Jaguar not been parked in the driveway, she doubted she would have known if she even still lived here, such was the deterioration of their relationship. The sad irony was that they didn't even live that far apart. Her mother's coastal home in the village of Seasalter was just a quarter of an hour's drive from her and Jacob's house in Faversham. Yet no chance meeting had occurred.

Evan had booked an hour with her mother as a patient at her practice a few years back so that she could try and explain about Jacob, but Vivian had refused to break professional character, and after an hour of listening to her daughter, she had offered professional advice and seen her on her way at the chime of the clock. Getting paid advice was never Evan's intention, and the point of the visit had been lost on her mother. One hour in six years wasn't enough for any child and parent.

The door opened slowly, as Vivian Phillips struggled with the security bolt while holding her phone to her ear. As soon as she saw who had knocked so firmly at her door, she found a way, in a language Evan guessed was German, to end the call.

'Evangeline!' said Vivian in a state of shock. 'I wasn't expecting...'

'Oh, just shut up, Mother,' said Evan, before wrapping her arms around her tightly. 'I know you don't do affection, but you are going to take this, and then you are going to get the kettle on. OK, Mum?' Evan went to let go but felt resistance.

'Are you sure you wouldn't prefer a glass of Pinot? I've just opened a little French number.'

Evan smiled at the unexpected warm reception and finally looked into her mum's eyes as she was released. 'Not today, Mum. Just a green tea will be fine, or one of those camomile ones that you used to hide at the back of the cupboard. Here, I'll make it.' She followed her mum into the kitchen, hoping that she would remember where everything was.

'No wine and you are offering to make the tea. Do I assume I need to muster some sort of ransom for the safe release of my actual daughter – you know, the one who usually has a more orange complexion and false lashes.'

'It's good to see that time hasn't taken your sense of sarcasm and wit away,' joked Evan as she finished filling the kettle. 'Listen, Mum, we need to clear the air. Will you sit and talk with me?'

'Of course, Evangeline. I would love to.'

'Don't call me that. No one has called me that for well over a decade. Christ, my husband nearly choked when he heard it on our

137

wedding day. He thought we were at the wrong wedding.'

'Your husband?'

Evan proudly lifted her wedding finger. 'Jacob and I were married nearly two years ago in a small ceremony in Tunbridge Wells. Don't tell me you have become so estranged and disconnected from my world that you didn't hear anything? I'm really sorry that you are only now just finding out, but I guess this is why we need to talk.'

'No, Evange… Evan. It's me who needs to apologise. I gave up hope of you ever forgiving my behaviour as an absentee mother and just accepted our paths to be different. Do I assume this to be the notorious Jacob Brooking?'

'I am officially Evan Laurie Brooking Phillips, and I can't hide the fact that I am both happier and more balanced than I have ever been because of him.'

'I can imagine he will say the same about you. How is he? How is his…' Vivian hesitated long enough for her daughter to interject.

'His mental health? Don't worry. He tells me everything. You should have seen his face though when he found out who you were in relation to me. I'm not sure any monster that has chased him through his dreams has ever scared him so much, and that's saying something, as I'm sure you know.'

'He's well, then?'

'He's really well. His bipolar really doesn't affect him too much since getting his medication right – well, unless he's stressed, but even that seems rare nowadays.'

'And his psychosis from the BPD?' asked Vivian, straying a little too close to full psychologist mode for Evan's liking.

'He hasn't heard a voice outside of his own in over a year, bar one incident when little Dorothy was poorly, but that was the exception that proves his recovery. It has taken some understanding on my part, but I went to a few classes on dealing with a mental health partner, and actually I find the whole thing quite interesting now. I start at the Open University next year, to do a degree in mental health nursing.'

'I'm not surprised that you have gone down that route at all.

You were always so very gifted; I just felt you lacked direction. I'm so happy you have found something you can embrace. So, my beautiful daughter is a stepmum. How is little Dorothy?'

'You won't believe this, but she's my best friend. I take her to dance class once a week and we fall asleep in front of a film nearly every Friday night. She is just amazing.'

'I don't know what to say. You turn up here, hardly any make-up on but looking more beautiful than ever before, you are married, a stepmum – and by all accounts an amazing one at that…'

'Is all this a bad thing?'

'Not at all. I just feel like you have done it all without me. It shows what an amazing woman you are, and honestly I take no credit for it.'

Evan took her mum's hand as a show of support. Vivian didn't cry, for it was not becoming of a woman of her stature, but Evan could see she was struggling.

'I didn't ever hate you because you were a bad mother. I hated you because I missed you, you were never there. But that doesn't mean you didn't teach me anything, and I loved you then just like I love you now.' Evan brushed the hair out of her mum's face and looked her square in the eyes. 'I won't forgive you because honestly that would mean looking backwards, and I only want to look forwards. That is something we do together or not at all.'

'Christ almighty, Evan. Now I know you are taking the piss, as that's one of my lines.'

'I did used to listen to you. I missed you so much that I used to break into your office as a kid and listen to your patient tapes, just so I could hear your voice.'

'Oh god, Evangeline Phillips, they were confidential,' said Vivian, laughing. 'So why now? Why do I deserve your presence in my life when I haven't earned it for many a year, if I ever earned it at all?'

'Because I need your help. I'm scared and I need my hand held through a few things.' She took her mum's hand and placed it on her belly. 'I'm pregnant, and as overjoyed as we both are, there are certain things men are useless at. An overexcited Jacob is a wonderful sight to behold, it wouldn't surprise me if he tried to deliver the little mite all on his own, but I need some female calm and composure in planning all this, if you know what I mean?'

'I'm going to be a grandmother,' said Vivian, with tears welling up in her eyes.

'Yes, Mum, you are.' Evan wrapped her arms around Vivian once more. 'We are going to be a family again.'

The lighthouse

'Wow, Ev, that is amazing,' said Jacob, gripping her hand tightly. 'I am so very proud of you. It is an enlightening thing to be able to move into our bright new world with that all left behind. You must be so happy to have your mum back in any capacity.'

'It will take time for us to find our way, of that I have no doubt. At our core, Mother and I are very different people in every respect, and it's been so long that we almost have to rebuild our friendship from scratch.' There was a melancholy in Evan's voice, but Jacob knew that his wife was feeling better for putting that particular demon to rest. 'Now, my deceptive little harlequin, what the hell is going on here? You wanted the rundown of my day in return for this devious plan you are clearly bursting to tell me, and you got it. So pull your fist out of your mouth and bloody tell me the script.'

'I guess now is as good a time as ever.' Jacob smiled. 'So, the lighthouse in front of you – well, I've bought it. It's ours. It belongs to us. It's –'

Evan jumped across the car and mounted Jacob in the passenger seat. 'Are you shitting me, Brooking, are you actually shitting me?'

'It's ours, and we can raise our little family right here. The lighthouse, the attached cottage, the holiday let at the rear and the annex, which I thought you could turn into an office for your studies and then eventually use as a clinic, if things go that way.'

Evan wasn't listening anymore. She was kissing Jacob between every word and, driven by pure passion, unbuttoning his trousers at the same time.

Jacob smiled at the elderly couple walking past. 'Let's get you inside for a look around, shall we, before we alienate the locals on the first day?'

Chapter 34:
Parlay and the Mourning Son

Song of the day: 'Wish You Were Here' by Pink Floyd

End of summer 2007

Psychiatric Hospital of San Diego County, California, USA

John Petalow gripped Jacob by the throat and pinned him against the wall of the hospital waiting room with such brute force that a calendar on the opposing wall fluttered to the ground.

'She's pregnant?' shouted John, blinded by rage. 'You bully my only child into trying to take her own life and you knock her up for good measure. Why? So she can't escape your narcissism. I should fucking kill you, Brooking.'

The Viking king might have been a huge man, but like most apex predators, knowing that he had no equal often meant he would forget to guard himself, and this was one of those times. Jacob wasn't the beast that his father-in-law was, but he was still a fairly fit young man who had been in enough scrapes in his life to know how to protect himself. You couldn't defend against a man like John Petalow for long, so instead Jacob drove a balled fist upwards, catching John on his chin with a thunderous uppercut that rocked him back a few feet. The Viking king wasn't a man who could be dropped by normal means, and even a punch of real quality wouldn't have come close to hurting him. In the aftermath of the incident, Jacob mused that his knuckles had taken more damage than John's face. However, something changed in John's eyes. A modicum of respect washed over him for just a moment, and he brought his hand up to his jaw and rotated it in a circular motion to check it wasn't damaged. Then he crossed his arms and uttered a single word: 'SPEAK!'

'I didn't bully her into anything. There is more to this than either of us understand, of that I am sure.' Jacob pulled himself straight. 'And, yes, I got my wife pregnant. That is something that can happen between two consenting adults, especially when they are husband and wife.'

'I warned you,' John growled. 'I told you to sort your life out.'

'And I have,' responded Jacob sharply. 'So stop jumping on my back. You may be Alice's father, but you damn sure are not mine.'

'So what do you intend to do here? Are you going to run away, like normal? Bury your head in the sand again?'

'I'll tell you what I'm going to do. When this child comes – which I have been assured can happen safely, whether Alice is awake or not – I will be as good a father as my own, and not a bully and a judgemental arsehole.'

John smiled at hearing Jacob fight back for a change. 'Careful there. Those are some big words you're throwing about, and I'd hate for you to break your other hand on my face.'

'I'm going to do right by her.'

'Her,' muttered the Viking king.

'It seems you are having a granddaughter – or should I say princess to your throne, my liege.' Jacob bowed theatrically as he spoke.

'Enough of that shit. I will only let so much go. Sit down.' John eased his giant frame into a plastic hospital chair and pointed to the one opposite. 'Listen, son, if you do what you say, I will give you my full support, as will my Angela. But I want something in return, and I promise you won't like it.' John leaned forward. 'We want you to leave Alice, and we want her home.' He raised his hand instantly to block the reply he knew was coming. 'Hear me out.

She's not happy, we both know that. But when was the last time you were happy? The last time you were not on the run? Alice is not the answer to your problems.'

Jacob sighed. 'I don't think that matters anyway. She found out about Evan and left me about three months ago. I say left me – kicked me out would be more precise. And, as you say, I did all I know how to do. I ran.'

'I guess that explains my friend's missing boat.'

Jacob nodded. 'Some weeks stuck afloat, then some spent getting my head right. I'm not the man you knew before. I'm not even the man Alice knew. But you're right. There is no happy ever after with us.'

'So we have a deal, son.' John offered his hand.

'Yeah, we have a deal. And any help moving forward would be greatly appreciated.'

'I'll talk to Angela as soon as we get back to the hotel.'

'What's wrong?' said Jacob, noticing how defeated John looked. 'Isn't this what you wanted?'

'My daughter in a coma, pregnant, divorcing her cheating husband… I'm not the monster you think I am. Let me tell you a secret.' He paused for a second. 'I mean what I've said, and I will honour our agreement to help you, but if you tell anyone what I'm about to tell you, I will gut you like a seabass. Not even Alice. OK?'

Jacob nodded, taken aback that his father-in-law, of all people, might tell him something that he wouldn't tell his own daughter.

'I have another child. In 1978 I had a one-night stand with someone I'd met through… well, it doesn't matter how we met. We never saw one another again – at least, she never saw me. I'd been with Angela for a few months when I saw this lady pushing a new-born baby. I knew it was mine. Don't ask me how I knew – just trust me. It was her baby, and it was mine.

'I was a coward. Instead of talking to her, I slipped away into the shadows in the hope that I never saw her again – a wish that came true. A wish that I have always regretted.'

Jacob couldn't find the words to convey his surprise. This story told of a man that he didn't know. Jacob realised that John hadn't always been so fearless.

'That's why I respect you in this,' said John, 'and that is why I am the father I am. I failed that child. I won't fail them both.'

'I get that. And thank you. I won't let any of you down in this, I promise.'

John rose quickly and placed a giant hand on Jacob's shoulder. 'I know you won't.'

As John walked away to give the news to his beloved wife, Jacob called out to him.

'John… I'm sorry that I punched you.'

John Petalow smiled but gave no reply. He didn't need to. He had made ground today with a young man he never thought he could respect for anything, and that was enough.

Autumn 2015

Jacob had been sitting on the tiny gardening stool opposite his father's memorial stone for two hours. The sun was setting, and it was turning colder. Yet he had found it impossible to leave his father's side. He felt comfort here, like he was with an old friend.

'I'm sorry, Dad. I'm sorry I couldn't mourn you when I should have, and I'm sorry I couldn't tell you this before.' Tears rolled down Jacob's cheeks. 'I have missed you so much since you left, and I cannot tell you how I have struggled to live up to the high standards you have set for me as a father, a son and a man. I have made so many mistakes in your absence, and with each one it has become more apparent that I've let you down.'

Jacob put his hand on his father's memorial stone and closed his eyes for a moment, as if to try and communicate his words through a more physical medium.

'I promise you now that I won't let them down like I have done you. I'm going to be better, and I'll make you so proud.' He opened his eyes and sat back down. 'You would be so proud of Sam too. He has these two boys that look the spit of you. Dotty looks like her mum, thank the lord, but she certainly has your spirit, which is enough for me. She would have loved you, Dad, just like we all still do.'

Jacob breathed out, and for the first time on that chilly Saturday afternoon, he felt a little better. He took to his feet, folding up the little stool that had been his perch, and headed back towards the car. He felt sadder than when he'd arrived, but less in turmoil as a result of his one-sided conversation.

'Are you OK, baby?' said Evan as Jacob came towards her.

'I'm good. More than that, actually – I'm truly happy.'

Evan reached for him and kissed him deeply on his cold lips. 'I'm so very proud of you.'

Jacob smiled. 'Proud of me? I'm proud of us, love. Look at how far we have come.' He looked over Evan's shoulder and into the back seat of his BMW. 'How is our little man?'

'Fast asleep at last. If I wake him for a feed when we get home, we might get him to sleep through.'

'I love you, Evan Brooking Phillips. Never change – just as you are is all I've ever wanted.'

'Aww, baby, do we need to look at moving your medication review? I know you have many, but I am not sure I've met this personality,' Evan joked, grabbing him tightly and kissing him passionately before he could form a smart reply.

They put their heads together one last time before a parting kiss saw Jacob head to the driver's seat.

'Let's get home,' said Evan as she slid into the passenger seat next to him.

'Goodbye, Dad, I'll see you soon,' said Jacob. He started the engine. 'He would have loved you, Evan.'

Evan placed her hand on his. 'He would have loved us.'

Chapter 35: Miss Palette

**Song of the day: 'Sign Your Name '
by Terence Trent D'Arby**

Autumn 2015

London, Kent, UK

The oil painting was hanging on the main wall of Blackberries auction house. Alice hadn't moved in over an hour, and the longer she looked at the painting, the more it seemed to look back at her. Alice thought of the philosopher Friedrich Nietzsche, who made the point that you couldn't stare into the abyss without the abyss staring back at you. The strokes of oil, both of light and of dark, certainly held that power over her right now. An almost hypnotic restraint kept her sitting painfully still as the girl within the strokes looked straight into her soul.

'It's an amazing piece,' said the tall man who had appeared out of nowhere and placed a hand on Alice's shoulder. 'But, sweet Jesus, it scares the life out of me.'

Aiden Hewett was the head auctioneer at Blackberries and commanded a great deal of respect within the professional circles that Alice kept.

'How are you, old friend?' asked Alice politely, raising her hand up to touch his.

'I am well, although I would be better if my friends would keep from referring to me as old.' Aiden, who was in his late fifties, had the angled look of an owl, with the slender frame of a marathon runner. His black turtleneck jumper only elongated his look further. 'I didn't know you were here in person; I know you had two pieces on sale today, but –'

'Three. I had three pieces on today. One was under the pseudonym of Angela Marie.'

'This is one of yours? Well, I must say, this is a departure from your usual style, and it has clearly worked for you. Why the change, may I ask?'

'It was my Dorian Gray, and it's a side of me that I didn't want to associate with my other work. My clientele back in Kent are a little on the pompous side.'

'That makes sense from a brand perspective, I guess,' said Aiden, taking a seat next to Alice, 'and explains you using... your mother's name?'

Alice nodded. 'She doesn't know, but I'm hoping she will take it as a compliment. You said my change in style had clearly worked for me, but I thought you weren't a fan of this particular piece?'

'I most certainly am not. But did you not watch your own auction today? Have you really just sat here, transfixed by the eyes of what looks like a lost version of yourself reflected within a mirror?'

'I'm sorry. You know how I hate watching my own work sell in front of a baying crowd. Did they all sell?'

Aiden reached into the leather satchel by his side and pulled out a piece of yellow paper, passing it to her with a smile. 'Your two normal pieces of work went for a little over your asking price of £2,000. And this monstrosity – well, what does your receipt say?'

'This can't be real?' Alice stared at the receipt, dumbstruck. 'I mean, I think this is my magnum opus, I truly believe that, but still – who would pay £250,000?'

'I believe the buyer was a Miss Palette. Part of an American gallery based out of Topeka in Kansas.'

'You are shitting me?' choked Alice with a chuckle.

'Miss Petalow – we don't use that language here. But, no, I am not "shitting" you.'

The girl in the painting watched them talk for a further half hour before two burly men covered her with a green felt blanket, took her from the wall and placed her securely into a crate. The painting, one made of tears, sweat and toil as well as canvas and oil, was a picture of a girl not unlike Alice. A girl haunted by her reflection, a girl frightened by something that would not leave her shadow, and a girl saddened by a world built on lies and the monster who sold them to her.

Chapter 36: Ripped from Reality

Song of the day: 'How Was it for You'
by Snowy White

Winter 2015

Whitstable, Kent, UK

'Dorothy, it's your holiday,' said Alice, who was doing a fine job of filing her nails in the comfort of her armchair while balancing the phone awkwardly on her shoulder.

'So you get to decide where we go next summer.'

'I know, Mum, but you deserve a holiday too. It's not been a quiet year for you, has it?'

'I love that you are thinking of me, but you are making this choice. You've got a few weeks yet, but it will obviously be cheaper the earlier we book it.'

'OK, keep your knickers on,' said Dorothy. 'I'm on it.'

'Say hello to your grandparents for me, would you? And Dorothy…'

'Yes, Mumma bear?'

'I love you, poppet.'

'I love you too, Mum. Sleep tight.'

Alice put the phone down and finished her nail maintenance before she got ready for bed. The apartment above her studio wasn't the biggest, but it had an almost regal feel to it. Original oak beams separated each room and Edwardian window frames gave a stunning view of the ocean. Alice loved the ocean dearly, for she slept so much better with its tide gently lapping against the empty oyster shells that littered the bay. Alice felt content within her home, within her life and within her world. It had been a long time coming, and with business getting ever busier, she knew it was only a matter of time before everything else clicked into place.

She washed her teeth in her en suite, her reflection looking back at her. She saw a few more wrinkles than normal and a grey hair or two hiding among her red locks, but she looked good. She looked more like her mum as she approached her forties, but then that was hardly a bad thing, as her mum was the most beautiful woman she knew. She rinsed her mouth out and gave herself a smile in her bathroom mirror before heading to bed. Her phone lit the room up with a jet of synthetic light and a small beep. Alice climbed into bed and reached across to where the phone lay.

How about Kansas? read the text from Dorothy. I hear the locals are friendly?

Alice smiled at the thought of seeing Poppy once more. They spoke daily, but she hadn't had the pleasure of her company since the after-party of her auction in London eight weeks before. The night had ended with a parting kiss that even on her best day Alice could not have explained.

A trip to the States would be great, Alice replied. I'll look into it tomorrow.

A loud knock at her front door woke Alice sharply. *Who the hell is that?* she thought. It was just after 7.30 a.m., although she felt like she had only just gone to bed. She held her throbbing head. The room was spinning. She rubbed her eyes and searched for her sense of reality. She had barely opened her eyes when she realised something wasn't right. Her apartment was fully carpeted, and yet as Alice slid out of bed, she felt only cold hard wood underneath her feet – the same floor that she'd had in her cottage all those years ago in her false reality.

I'm not buying into this. I've been doing this far too long, thought Alice with an inner chuckle. She was far too used to being exposed to the false realities that her broken brain would invent.

'Are you OK, Papillon?'

Alice turned in shock – shock but not fear, as she knew that in this place, there was nothing substantial to fear. William looked back at her. He rubbed his neck with both hands before pulling his chiselled body upright.

'I know you can't be real, but, damn, what a pleasant surprise,' Alice said with thirsty excitement, before she leaned in and kissed him passionately. She knew he wasn't anything other than a fiction created by her cruel brain, but she had missed seeing his face.

William pulled away after two more deep kisses ended with Alice mounting him and pulling at his boxers.

'What on earth has got into you?' said William, both confused and aroused in equal measure. 'This isn't the wake-up call I was expecting.'

'God, you even smell the same. I will say this, my mind really has an eye for detail when it comes to fucking me over, doesn't it?' Alice went back in to finish the job she had started on William before the loud knock at the door hit once again. 'Hold on, baby. They are clearly not going to let us alone. I'll just play the game, I guess. After all, I'm usually brought here for a reason. But you'd better still be here when I return, my handsome but imaginary man.'

Alice rolled off of William's flustered body and, remembering her way through her old imaginary home, made her way to the top of the stairs.

'Oh my,' said Alice. 'This is new.'

She was at least seven months pregnant.

'Wow, I could get used to this,' Alice cooed, rubbing her baby bump. 'It's not real, Pebble. Just enjoy the moment, you daft cow.'

There was another knock on the door.

'Hold your horses. I'm bloody coming. Don't you know I'm carrying a child here?'

Alice struggled to the bottom of the stairs and opened the door.

'Alice – sorry, I know it's early, but I need –'

'It had to be you. My bloody mind couldn't leave me upstairs with William, could it? Please continue, Evan. Honestly, no dream is fit for purpose without you trying to screw me over.'

'I just need to talk to you about something. Can I come in?'

'Please, Your Majesty, come through to the kitchen.' Alice made a regal gesture of welcome. 'Tell me, will Our Royal Highness be joining us, or have you left Jacob alone in bed at home?'

Evan walked through to the kitchen and placed her hands on the sink, almost bracing herself for the conversation ahead. 'I don't even know how to start this without sounding crazy, but I hope you at least understand my intention for coming here and that you see it's not to hurt you.'

Alice had moved to within inches of her without making a sound, and Evan looked down to see a large kitchen knife buried in her abdomen, pushed to the handle. The blood being released was minimal, but as Evan's body went into survival shock, she knew that pulling the knife out would drastically change that.

'Alice, what have you...?'

Alice drew herself closer and strengthened her grip on the handle. 'Don't you "Alice" me. You know you had this coming, and if this false reality is the only place that I'm free to do it, then so be it.'

That felt good. You know it's not real, so do it again.

'I've needed this psychosis of mine to work for me for a change,' said Alice, twisting the knife, 'and I have to be honest, it feels so good that I'm tempted to do it in the real world.'

Now get back up to William, before you wake up. Alice pushed Evan to the ground and turned about with a swagger, only to find Jacob standing there, pale with horror. He rushed over to Evan and pulled a pile of kitchen towels from the counter.

'WHAT HAVE YOU DONE, ALICE?' he screamed. He drew the knife out of Evan's belly, using the towels to stem the blood loss.

Why do they all rush to her side all the time?

'Come on, Jay, William's upstairs, so let's not waste what little time we have together. She doesn't even exist, a bit like you, really, but if I have to be stuck here, I would rather be upstairs with you.'

'Alice, she is going to die here in my arms if you don't call an ambulance, so CALL A FUCKING AMBULANCE!'

Might as well give up on this. Once again it's turned to shit. My mind clearly hates me. Alice closed her eyes and clenched her fists in an act of frustration.

'Alice,' cried Evan.

Alice opened her eyes and realised she was still in the cottage kitchen. *Focus, Pebble, you've got this.* Again, she closed her eyes and clenched her fists tightly.

'Alice, you're…'

Chapter 37: Epilogue

The creature still existed, but somehow the girl Alice had taken its mask away. It had no form to physically manifest into now, but it still existed as an entity, still watched her and wished for nothing but tragedy to befall her miserable fake life. The creature knew it had to wait, though, knew it didn't have the power to raise its voice right now, so it didn't have a chance of getting her attention, let alone of hurting her. Something would happen to give the creature strength, it always did, as was the very essence of life. For now, the mirrored demon self of Alice Petalow would be patient, a trait that it didn't normally possess.

It climbed into a selection of bad memories – one of Thomas, one of a murdered child and one of a cheating husband – and it closed its eyes to accept the sleep of the wicked, the sleep that it needed, and it wondered if it would dream like the girl Alice would dream.

The creature closed its metaphorical mind's eye and hoped that it would dream. But as it drifted off, onto a plane of existence outside of hate and jealousy, there was nothing.

In the waking world, Alice looked down at the carnage in front of her that wouldn't disappear.

The End

Coming soon

Before the Viking King

Book 3 in the Broken Pebbles series
Coming November 2020

The South Atlantic

February 1977

Quote of the day: 'The best weapon against an enemy is another enemy.' – Friedrich Nietzsche

John awoke to the sound of bending steel and the aching frame of the pressure-filled mechanical monstrosity that he had called home for the past three months. It wasn't the painful cries of the submarine that scared him – actually, those sounds were a welcome reminder that he was still alive. It was the lack of any human noise. Where is everyone? he thought as he rose up from the infirmary bed, feeling nauseous from decompression sickness. Submarines were notorious for being constantly busy, almost like an ant colony. Corridors laced the ship, each as narrow as the next, and there was only so much room even for the skeleton crew that manned the HMS Oberon. It wasn't unusual to have three people trying to pass you at the same corridor junction, all in a rush to complete an important task. But his small unit of frogmen, a team of six seasoned warriors, were absent as he searched around the infirmary.

'Hello?' he called down the corridor that attached to the main infirmary door, but no reply was forthcoming, and, worse than that, he could hear nothing at all, not a whisper, just the constant groan of the ship as it toiled in pain. The corridors often acted as an instrument to carry sound from one end of the boat to the other, but this time they brought only the aching sound of the hull as it screeched under the pressure of the ocean. Realising that he was still in an open-back gown, John made his way out of the medical bay, heading through the lower section of the boat, towards the bunks that C Squadron had made their home. It was not a short journey, and he was worried that he would run into someone with his arse hanging out, which would lead to the boys having a good laugh at him for sure. They always did, regardless of whether they had an excuse or not. He was the youngest of C Squadron's elite. In fact, he was the youngest swimmer canoeist to pass the UK Special Forces selection and had only recently transferred from his home at 45 Commando in Arbroath down to the Special Boat Service in Poole. It was a move that, if nothing else, meant his winters would not be so mind-numbingly cold, although mind-numbingly cold was something his rear end was feeling as he moved quickly across the steel-grate floor barefoot and with a bare back.

At first he moved with absolute stealth so as to avoid being caught half-naked, but his desire to kitten-crawl through the whole ship began to wane as he realised that his feeling of solitude wasn't unfounded. He was completely alone. Could everyone be on top deck? Had they docked? *Where the fuck is everyone?* he repeated over and over as he entered the shared bunk, dropped his gown to the floor, grabbed a navy-blue T-shirt from his trunk and pulled it on. John continued to curse the rest of his team as he struggled to get the marine-issue combat trousers over his thighs. He may have been the youngest, but he was easily the muscliest of the group. While the rest of the team were lithe and streamlined for swimming and long-distance tabbing, John was built like a shire horse.

He holstered his Browning L9 pistol to his leg and ran a hand through his auburn hair. 'Right, Petalow, let's see what's going on here.'

He entered the corridor from his box room, and as the lights flickered and then failed, he had an overwhelming feeling that he was walking into his own worst nightmare. After several seconds of total darkness, emergency bulbs threw a red shade over the desolation that littered the floor. The crimson light highlighted a reality that John could not even begin to comprehend. The floor, which just minutes ago was as empty as the infirmary he had woken up in, was now littered with dead submariners, each of them with sunken eyes that stared at the celling as if pleading with God for help. John knelt down next to the closest body, an able seaman by the name of Julian Carrol. His memories of the poor chap were sparse, but John had been in awe of Julian's team and looked at them like they were real-world superheroes. 'What's happened to you, little buddy?' said John as he tried to find a pulse in Julian's cold-skinned corpse. Lance Corporal John Petalow had seen dead bodies before. Not only that – he had killed men. Death wasn't something he feared. But he'd never seen this before, a dozen dead bodies appearing outside his door as if from nowhere.

Instinct kicked in. His heart rate picked up and his right hand hovered over his holster.

Pick up the pace, Johnny boy. Or do you want to sleep in the shed again, you little bastard?

John's hand instinctively found his pistol, and within the blink of an eye, he had it half drawn and the safety removed.

'Who's there?' he shouted.

You always were the slow one, said the voice, as the plethora of bodies all turned their heads to face him with dead and lifeless eyes.

He felt sick as he put his finger on the trigger of his sidearm, but his training couldn't prepare him for what he was seeing, or for the voice that he was hearing.

'Father?' he called out.

Cairo, Egypt

February 1977

Quote of the day: 'There are only two tragedies in life: one is not getting what one wants, and the other is getting it.' – *Oscar Wilde*

Laurie Rosenberg couldn't believe her luck as she watched Vivian go through the bazaar meticulously smelling and tasting all the different spices available. Yesterday it was silks and fine cotton, today cured meats and ground herbs. Laurie could watch her all day long. Vivian had always seemed so curious about everything; her eyes were wide and her thirst for boundless adventure was forever unsatisfied.

They were dressed in kaftan-style robes, Laurie's an emerald green and Vivian's the finest golds of Egypt. Bracelets and bangles adorned Vivian's wrists and gave her an almost Hindu vibe that put Laurie in mind of the George Harrison song 'My Sweet Lord'. Her style was what made her stand out in the crowd, but it was her inquisitive mind that kept Laurie coming back for more. Vivian Phillips was her brightest student and now her soulmate. Laurie was unsure how this had happened, but she was happy it had. There would be hell to pay upon their return to England. Professor Laurie Rosenberg was no more. She had already been told that her job was to be taken from her, although that was actually the least of her concerns in relation to going back. The fallout from Andrew's family would be horrific. They were a bunch of snotty braggards and would do their very best to ruin her reputation. What chance was there that they would believe a small-town girl like her over a violent and narcissistic son, one who was cut from the very same cloth as them? *We will deal with it together*, Vivian had said, as she fought to reassure Laurie. *Who cares what they say or even think for that matter?* She was right, but it wasn't every day that Laurie left an abusive marriage to run across the world with one of her students whom she had fallen madly in love with.

Vivian appeared in front of her and forced a chilli-infused tiger prawn into her mouth. 'How amazing is that? Isn't it just so… so… recherché.'

Laurie had to finish chewing the thing before she answered, but she couldn't deny its elegance as the heat danced off her tongue.

'I wish I'd never taught you that word,' she groaned. 'But, yes, it's incredibly "recherché".'

Vivian leaned in and kissed Laurie, feeling the heat from the chilli once more as it danced from one set of lips to another. 'Darling, I've been thinking.'

'Oh shit, that's not good. Do I need to sit down?' joked Laurie with a lick of her lips, before taking Vivian by the hand. 'I know what you've been thinking, and, yes, I think it's time to go home.'

'How did you know? I mean, I know that you are my mirror, but still… Have I been that obvious in my desires?'

'You talk about home in your sleep, Viv. That and I'm a trained psychologist. Or had you forgotten?' Laurie brought Vivian's hand up to her mouth and kissed it with a delicate purse of her lips. 'I want to go home too. I'm just not sure where to find the courage to do it.'

'Whatever happens, we will always be by one another's side. We owe each other that much. We promised each other, or had you forgotten?'

'How could I forget, my love?' said Laurie with a final kiss before Vivian jumped back into her excited child persona, going from one market stall to the next.

Laurie was scared, but she was content, for she knew that as long as they had each other, nothing else mattered.

The End

Printed in Poland
by Amazon Fulfillment
Poland Sp. z o.o., Wrocław

57826680R00103